Sarah Fermi has been interested in the Brontë family for almost as long as she can remember. Perhaps being one of three sisters may have been the starting point, but her serious interest was prompted by reading a biography of Emily Brontë by Edward Chitham. Inspired by his pertinent (and unanswered) questions about Emily, Sarah has devoted nearly fifteen years to examining the many previously unexplored personal connections of the Brontë sisters.

The controversial theory on which this book is based was taken up by BBC Radio 4, and the play 'Cold in the Earth, and Fifteen Wild Decembers', by Sally Wainwright, was the result. It was broadcast in March, 2006, as the Saturday Afternoon Play.

EMILY'S JOURNAL

SARAH FERMI

EMILY'S JOURNAL

**With annotations by her Sisters,
Charlotte and Anne Brontë**

Edited by Charlotte Brontë

Sarah Fermi

Pegasus

PEGASUS PAPERBACK
© Copyright 2006
Sarah Fermi

A CIP catalogue record for this title is
available from the British Library

ISBN-13: 978 1903490 25 9
ISBN-10: 1 903490 25 1

*Pegasus is an imprint of
Pegasus Elliot MacKenzie Publishers Ltd.*
www.pegasuspublishers.com

Cover image is the work of the author who was inspired by the portrait
of Emily by Patrick Branwell Brontë in the National Portrait Gallery.

The source of the maps is the 1852 Ordinance Survey of the West
Riding of Yorkshire, 6 miles to the inch, reproduced by kind permission
of the Syndics of Cambridge University Library.

First Published in 2006

**Pegasus
Sheraton House Castle Park
Cambridge England**
Printed & Bound in Great Britain

In memory of my late husband,
who told me fifteen years ago
that I should write this book.
Well, Judd, here it is at last.

Acknowledgements and thanks:

A great number of people have contributed directly or indirectly to the creation of *Emily's Journal*: Hazel Holmes, Robin Greenwood, Dorinda Kinghorn, Ann Dinsdale, Judith Smith, Diane and Robert Ware, Dr Heather Glen, Tamsin and Douglas Palmer, Dr Gillian Jondorf, Harriet Jondorf, Julie Ackhurst, Brenda Taylor, Rebecca Fraser, Polly Teale and Caroline Davidson. Some of these people have read the manuscript during its development and given helpful comments, some have contributed deep background material for the social background of Haworth in the 1830s and '40s, and several have done both. The BBC has been indirectly involved in the writing of *Emily's Journal* as the theory underlying the book was taken up by BBC Wales (producers Karen Lewis and Deborah Perkin) and Sally Wainwright was commissioned to write a drama script based on my research; in fact this book began as a research aid for Sally. In the end the play was not filmed for television but was adapted for radio by Sally and was produced and directed by Pauline Harris.

I particularly want to thank Dr Patsy Stoneman who has been my friend and advisor from the earliest inception of the theory right up to the finished manuscript of the book, and who has kindly provided the Preface to this edition. Without her the book would probably never have been written.

Sarah Fermi
Cambridge
July 2006

Preface by Patsy Stoneman

It is more than fifteen years since, in the course of a stormy walk to Ponden Kirk, Sarah Fermi first held me enthralled with her theory about Robert Clayton, the boy who could have been the object of Emily Brontë's love. Since then, Sarah has published no fewer than seven scholarly articles untangling various mysteries in the lives of Haworth families. These articles are now cited as reliable evidence by authorities in the field – biographers and editors of the Brontë letters. Sarah's methods are those of the traditional historian: the patient and meticulous sifting of church records, land registers, wills and testaments, and, where they exist, letters and memoirs. By these means she has been able to solve problems which have lain uninvestigated since Gaskell's *Life of Charlotte Brontë*.

The vital piece of evidence which might link Robert Clayton with Emily Brontë still, however, eludes her, and may, in fact, not exist, since the Clayton family were poor farmers and weavers, and, being probably illiterate, would have left no written records. Sarah's theory, however, already has a more solid foundation than any other attempt to find a lover for Emily Brontë. Robert Clayton was a real person, born within weeks of Emily Brontë and living where she could have easily encountered him in her walks on the moors. His birth is recorded in Haworth Church, and so, crucially, is his death, at the age of eighteen, at the very point in Emily's life when her poetry began its intense focus on death and bereavement.

Sarah belongs to that group of readers who are powerfully convinced that Emily Brontë must have had a real live lover in order to write *Wuthering Heights,* and she set out deliberately to discover a person whose death might underlie Emily's pervasive obsession with bereavement. Intending systematically to investigate all the young men in the Haworth area who died at about the right time, she found that Robert was the only one.

By contrast, I had never felt that personal experience was essential to imaginative writing. It seemed to me that the Brontë juvenilia demonstrate how intensely imagination can inhabit situations which the writer has not experienced in person. Reading Shelley and Byron in her early teens, I thought, Emily could have reproduced their passion as if it were her own. What gave me pause, and made me feel that this theory deserved serious attention, was the fact that Robert Clayton's death, at a known date, marks with uncanny precision the onset of Emily's intense poems of grief and loss. Having previously read these poems as a loose collection of meditations on imaginary states of mind, I found that Sarah's theory transformed them into a terse, focused cycle, an elegy for lost love.

During the years while Sarah was searching for her clinching evidence, she became intimately knowledgeable about the dating of events in the Brontë lives, and had the leisure to imagine the impact of a relationship such as this on the lives of the whole family. Despairing of the proven fact, she decided to flesh out her theory with fiction based as accurately as possible on verifiable evidence. Her sketch attracted the attention of the BBC, who commissioned a script by the television writer, Sally Wainwright. Sadly, the drama itself was never commissioned, but Sally went on to adapt the play for Radio 4, and it was broadcast as 'Cold in the Earth, and Fifteen Wild Decembers' on 11 March, 2006, as a Saturday play.

Sarah never felt, however, that a play could adequately render the minute detail in which such a relationship would have affected Emily's life and writing, and so she began working out this detail in the form of Emily's (fictitious) journal. The real Emily Brontë did not, of course, leave a journal and much of the book you are about to read is the product of Sarah Fermi's imagination. *Emily's Journal* is thus a controversial book, and doubtless some readers will react against it. Where it differs profoundly, however, from most of the Brontë 'spin-offs' which crowd the bookshop shelves is that wherever a fact can be checked against the best available evidence, it will be found to be accurate. Brontë enthusiasts reading *Emily's Journal* may recoil from its radical propositions, but they will not be offended by impossible coincidences of dates, or places, or persons. No-one can say whether the events recounted here did happen, but as far as the facts are known, they *could* have happened.

Dr Patsy Stoneman, reader emeritus in English, the
University of Hull
June 2006

Foreword

Many biographies of Emily Brontë have appeared over the past 130 years; a fascination with the mysterious author of *Wuthering Heights* and a handful of intensely moving poems shows no sign of abating. Although most of these biographies vary considerably in style and viewpoint, most have some kind of theory about her — what she was like, and why she wrote in the manner she did. Only one element unites these books and that is the admission that very little is actually known of Emily's life. Yet most of them claim to be factual and therefore, implicitly, to give an accurate picture of that life. We are even warned in the more 'responsible' works that 'there is so little external material that the temptation to use imagination is strong' (Edward Chitham, *A Life of Emily Brontë*, 1987). Winifred Gérin in her *Emily Brontë* (1971) says: 'The scarcity of direct evidence relating to her and the mystery that has been allowed to surround her life, while enhancing her appeal for writers, has tempted them to produce unauthenticated narratives and to invent where they could not record'. Lucasta Miller's *The Brontë Myth (2001)* echoes the same sentiment: 'The absences surrounding [Emily] have made her all the more magnetic, and some colourful apocrypha has emerged to fill the gaps'.

But the 'gaps' are the root of the problem. Here is where the real story must lie. The truth is that the few confirmed facts of Emily Brontë's life simply do not add up to a coherent picture. The enormous 'gap' between what is known of her life and the extraordinary nature of her work (both her novel, *Wuthering Heights*, and her poetry) points inexorably to the probable existence of some unrecorded but formative event or events which would begin to explain the hidden 'secret pleasure, secret tears'* which appear to be the wellsprings of her work.

Since no properly-documented biography of Emily *can* be written, simply because there are not enough facts on record to justify one, there seemed to me to be only one alternative: this was to explore the question from the other end. I have adopted a risky and unorthodox plan of attack and *started* from the point of view that Emily Brontë wrote *Wuthering Heights* for a real reason, from some sort of personal necessity, and that something *must* have happened to her in her youth to explain the enigma of the origins of the book and the passion of the poetry.

Accordingly, I went back and looked again at those few paltry documentary facts. Did they make sense? Were there gaps and contradictions in them? Looking at the problems with these shreds of evidence it became clear that they might indeed conceal an unknown story. For example, as a child Emily was charming and outgoing, if the evidence from her entry in the Clergy Daughters' School register is to be believed. Yet in later years she is known to have been reserved, almost reclusive. Why? In 1835, at the advanced age of 17, Emily was suddenly sent off to school, apparently against her will, and at a time when the family's limited funds were needed to send her brother Branwell to the Royal Academy Schools in London. Why? No reason has ever been given to explain this illogical step. Furthermore, her father wrote to a family friend at this time about his worries over Emily's youth and inexperience, and the temptations of 'this delusive and ensnaring world'. So why was he sending her away, and on very short notice? Emily nearly died at the school, and was sent home within three months. Can this be attributed to home-sickness, as her sister Charlotte later claimed, or was there a deeper, more personal reason for her distress? Then there is the high frequency in her poetry of poems referring to an early lost love — although some of these are

---

* This is the first line of the second verse of a poem written in May, 1839, which begins, 'I am the only being whose doom/ No tongue would ask, no eye would mourn...' The whole second verse reads, 'In secret pleasure, secret tears,/ This changeful life has slipped away,/ As friendless after eighteen years,/ As lone as on my natal day.'

apparently poems which form part of her and Anne's fictional Gondal sagas, many of them are specifically personal works and were transcribed into her notebook of non-Gondal poetry. The general outline of a picture begins to emerge from these suggestive 'facts': was Emily sent away to school to break off an unsuitable relationship? Did the boy die or disappear sometime soon after? Did she mourn him for the rest of her life?

Taking this brief outline of a possible life-altering experience sometime in the 1830s, I reread all her poetry in chronological order, and was struck by the abrupt change in tone between 1836 and 1837. In December, 1836, she wrote probably her only really joyous poem ('High waving heather...') then nothing until February, 1837, when the tone is suddenly darker and deeply melancholy. Could the death or disappearance of a young lover at this time explain the change? Since many of Emily Brontë's poems about a young lost love involved his death (though there are a few about his departure), I decided this was the most likely scenario and, hopefully, there would be a record of such a death in the Haworth Burial Records for 1836 – 37. To my amazement, I found one likely candidate. He was Robert Clayton, a working-class lad, exactly the same age as Emily (born in July, 1818), who was buried by Patrick Brontë on the 14th of December, 1836. Further research turned up several other interesting facts about him and his family which appeared to confirm my suspicions. Probably the most significant one was the death of Robert's older brother John in 1833. One of Emily's greatest poems ('Death that struck when I was most confiding...') appears to refer to two related deaths, one which barely touched her, but the other destroyed her. This poem is quoted in full on page 146. Another small piece of suggestive evidence is that the initials 'A.E. and R.C.' appear alongside one of her fictional Gondal poems. Although A.E. probably refers to the Gondal character, Alexander Elbë, the initials R.C. do not appear to correspond to any known Gondal character. I wondered if perhaps Robert might once have acted the part of Alexander in the early days (1831 – 35) when the stories were being acted out on the moors by Anne and Emily. This seemed not only possible but likely from another point of view — it might explain why Emily continued to pursue the Gondal stories long after Anne had tired of them. Furthermore, Alexander Elbë's death is recorded, unusually, in three poems by Emily, and indeed he never appears as a living character in any of the other Gondal poems.

Of course, I cannot ultimately prove that any relationship existed between Emily Brontë and Robert Clayton. The chances of finding documentary evidence of something which all parties would probably have tried to conceal is unlikely in the extreme. The one person to write about Emily who actually could have known the secrets of her life was her sister Charlotte. But nothing Charlotte says about Emily can be fully relied upon — the picture she paints of her strange sister ('a homebred country girl') is full of omissions, contradictions and actual inaccuracies, all in aid of defending Emily from accusations of vulgarity, coarseness and immorality after the publication of *Wuthering Heights*. One would hardly expect her to reveal in print that her sister had been disgraced when she was only 17 because of a socially unsuitable relationship with a poor weaver's son.

Because I cannot document any part of my rather extensive theory about Emily's life, but am convinced it is both plausible and compelling, I found the only way to write about it was to present it in the form of a story. The idea of writing it as if written by Emily Brontë herself in the style of her own occasional journal, and with comments on the entries written by her sisters, Anne and Charlotte, after Emily's death in 1848, allowed me to work from the inside out, so to speak, and I found it was possible not only to convey more convincingly the basic elements of the theory, but also to see and connect certain events in Emily and her sisters' lives in a new way, one which was far more instructive than simply the recording of events.

The writing of this book has been, in a way, a kind of experiment; I have tried to juggle all that I know about the Brontës — their works, their lives, not to mention all my own research into the families of Haworth — in an effort to find out how all these things would fit with the theory of Emily's alleged disastrous connection with young Robert Clayton. Because every imaginative reconstruction of events contained in these pages is based on either fact, circumstantial evidence, historical context, or plausible theory, and every person described really lived in the time, place, and manner described, it seems to me that the whole speculative endeavour tends to suggest a degree of authenticity — it all seems to hang together and to make sense.

In the end, the intention of this book is to present a new point of view on the life of this most secretive and private author. Although my story cannot be true in every detail, I hope it plausibly suggests that Emily Brontë had a close and tragic relationship in her adolescence which haunted the rest of her life and which provided much of the material for her great novel and many of her most moving poems.

'EJB – her book'

Introduction

When the several manuscript notebooks of this precious Journal were handed to me by my sister Anne early in this year 1849, only a few months had passed since my sister Emily had been taken to her final rest. A few months more, and Anne too would be called to her long home. Thus these little books were our last brief remaining contact with her, whom we both loved above all others. I will ever be grateful to Anne, who was failing daily, for sharing this deeply personal document with me, as I know the pain she must needs have experienced in doing so. But she felt that we would both benefit from this window into Emily's very private world, and that we would derive strength from her example and understanding from her honesty.

In that precious interval of time, while the increasing signs of Anne's illness showed too clearly that she would not linger long on this Earth, our shared reading of this Journal opened to us a past we had thought lost for ever, recalling from the dead our beloved sister, who had hastened to leave us.

All during the months of January and February we pored over every entry, making our own written observations on the events and thoughts described therein. At that time I gave no thought to what would become of these papers, but only felt impelled to add my voice to hers, to relive as nearly as possible our lives together and apart. Some of this work has been painful in the extreme (Emily was always forthright with her opinions), but I own I feel the better for it.

During those bleak months of winter and early spring, the Journal was our sole interest. Anne was too ill to indict a new novel; my own new work, *Shirley*, was at a complete standstill — all my ideas were in a tumult, and no effort of mine could bring them into any order. The Journal was for both of us a kind of lifeline, and I can attribute the final completion of *Shirley* by the end of this past summer to its healthful influence. For Anne, of course, the Journal represented only a nostalgic coda to her short life.

After Anne's death in May of this year, I considered

burning the Journal and all our notes and comments. Emily had asked Anne to do this, and Anne had begged me to destroy everything. But I found I could not. I am now virtually alone in the world, bereft of my siblings, my father is ailing, and even dear old Tabitha Aykroyd, our faithful servant, is declining. The house is silent, filled with the memories of the dead. How could I commit to the flames this last reflected glimmer of their bright selves?

So I decided at length that not only would I never burn these papers, I would prepare them for the distant possibility that one day the great reading public may wish to know more about Anne and Emily Brontë, both talented writers of prose, and one a great poet. That time is still very far off, but some day, when all our acquaintance have passed on to the next world, when the truth can no longer hurt friend or foe, I believe with all my heart that their works will still be read and that some readers may be interested to know more about their blameless lives.

In transcribing this Journal I have taken the liberty of correcting Emily's spelling and punctuation, but I have left the words as she wrote them, and I have added nothing beyond my and Anne's clearly identified comments, and a few footnotes where the text required clarification or further comment. I have also included Anne's pathetic last entries, painful as they are to myself, and my own final remarks after her death, written when I was still determined to burn the entire production. I hope Emily and Anne will forgive me for not doing so.

C. Brontë
Haworth Parsonage
15 October, 1849

Today is Charlotte's 15th birthday, and I begin this Journal in honour of her. She has been away at school now for three months. When she comes home in June, she can read this and know what we have all been doing while she was away.

Anne and I have tried to keep up the Young Men's Magazine, but Branwell refuses to help us, and as neither of us can write as small as Charlotte or Branwell, we have given it up. Branwell is getting to be more of a rare lad every day. He is out and about with his friends as often as possible. Last month his voice began to break and we had to laugh when he was reading his new poem to us (called an Ode in Praise of the Twelves)[*] and on the line, 'and all our crimes and our transgressions own...' it jumped down an octave on the last syllable of 'transgres-<u>sions</u>'. Since then he has stopped reading aloud to anyone!

Most of our time is taken up with lessons now, so we don't get too far behind Charlotte. Aunt Branwell is still teaching us plain and fancy sewing; it is wearisome work, very tiring. Much more interesting is cooking, but Aunt (who is an excellent cook) and Tabby only let us help with the menial labour. Papa teaches Branwell by himself (Latin and Greek). I wonder what Charlotte is learning? She says in her letters that she is learning a great deal, especially French and drawing and history, and also that she has made friends at Roe Head. I hope she will not forget us. We miss her so much, life seems drab without her.

Anne and I have started to work out a new game to play. It carries on from one we used to play (The Islanders) and takes place at the Palace of Instruction. Once we all played this game (we were the little king and queens) but

---

[*] It would take many pages to fully explain 'The Twelves', so I will simply state that they were nothing more than wooden toy soldiers, but we imbued them with the characters of our earliest heroes, and all our subsequent games and stories began with them.

now of course it's just me and Anne. We haven't worked out very much yet, only that I am going to be a Princess and Anne will be my lady-in-waiting, and we will both be pupils at the Palace of Instruction. I want it to be full of magic and such like, but Anne also wants to put in some romantic entanglements. But first we need to decide in what country am I a Princess, and why we are at school.

Papa has been very ill this winter, but he is now much recovered. While he was confined to his bed, he liked to have me read to him (I read aloud better than Anne or Aunt) and together we read all of the final part of Sir Walter Scott's Tales of a Grandfather. I know Papa feels very close to Sir Walter, and we both love his little grandson, Hugh Littlejohn, for whom the book was written.

Nothing else of importance has happened since January. We all miss Charlotte and long for her return home in June.

Emily Jane Brontë

Darling Emily, I will always remember your shining face and bonny laughter as we planned our next adventure together. Pray God that we shall meet again in a better place.

A. Brontë
31 December, 1848

Anne has just allowed me to read this amazing Journal. I must admit I began reading with great trepidation; I greatly feared that it would contain matter painful to me, but so far I find that the Journal is very like Emily herself — honest, brave, and on the whole, cheerful. I have read and reread this first entry several times, and I have no words to convey how deeply it affects me. Emily was at that time such a happy, joyous child. Now she is no more. How can we go on without her...?

C. Brontë
30 January, 1849

I began this journal two years ago. I meant to write in it frequently, while Charlotte was away, but nothing much happened and then she came home again, so there didn't seem much point and I didn't even bother to show it to her. Then I forgot about it. And in the summer of last year she came home for good. Since then much of interest has happened, but it is mainly secret, so that I have decided to go on with writing this journal, just for my own pleasure, and for my audience of imaginary readers. I like to picture them as airy elves and fairies, peering over my shoulder as I write, whispering amongst themselves in their strange language. Well, my friends, this is what happened in Anno Domini 1831 and 1832:

As I mentioned in my first entry, Anne and I started playing our new games by ourselves in the spring of 1831 — Branwell had made new friends and thought we were useless as we always wanted to play games while he wanted to write or paint or go out with his friends. Our story is all about an island country called Gondal. It is located in the North Pacific Ocean. We usually went out on the moors to play out the dramatic scenes (when the weather permitted), but we also had bed plays as we now share the back bedroom — Branwell must have his own room now — Aunt Branwell decided it is not suitable for a 'young man' of fourteen to sleep in the same room as his sisters, and he must have his own private space, so he was moved into the Children's Study over the stairs. After Maria and Elizabeth died (they had shared the Study) their room became a haven for the four of us, and the bedroom was only for me and Charlotte and Branwell to sleep in (Anne slept in Aunt's room at that time). But when Charlotte went away, Anne and I took over the bedroom to ourselves, which was delightful, and Branwell is mightily pleased to have the Study all to himself.

The idea for the Gondal stories came from our own English princess, Victoria, who is only a year younger than me, and who will one day be Queen of England. The heroine of our history is the Princess Augusta, who will ascend the

9

throne of Gondal when she attains the age of 18, all being well. She is sent away to school to be educated in the arts of painting, music, history, and, of course, politics, and is accompanied by her dear friend and lady-in-waiting, the Lady Juliet. But there are plots afoot to prevent her being crowned — the Republicans want to rid Gondal of its monarchy and are preparing for a bloody revolution, and at the same time, Augusta's evil uncle (her dead father's brother) wants to take the throne for himself. And his son (her cousin) Gerald, also at the Palace of Instruction, is her sworn enemy as he supports his father's claim. But I am getting ahead of my story.

The great secret event of 1831 happened at the end of the summer, just before my 13th birthday. Anne and I were sent to deliver some letters for Papa to the Church Trustees who live out in Stanbury (that's a village in our township just west of Haworth). After we'd stopped by the Taylors and the Crabtrees, and were on our way up to Ponden House (that's the big house on the edge of the moors where the Heatons live, about half a mile further on from Stanbury) we nearly collided with the Clayton boys coming down from the moors. Looking back, it was a fateful moment, but of course we couldn't know that then.

Anne and I had been discussing the next episode in our new story, and Anne was cross because I wanted her to play the villain, Gerald. She hates playing the boys' parts, especially if they are nasty. So I had a brilliant idea. Why not ask the Clayton boys if they'd like to play our game with us. It seemed to me that there was no harm in asking. They looked like intelligent fellows — nothing ventured, and so forth. Well, at first John was very sarcastic, and said they were too busy working, and wouldn't want their friends to see them playing with girls, especially not with the Parson's daughters. But I was very clever and started telling them the story and describing the sort of parts they might play. And when I told them about the plots and intrigues and sword fights and maybe even a great school rebellion, they began to be interested, even though neither of them has ever been to school. And the younger one, Robert, seemed truly enchanted by the whole idea. The older one, John, was more reluctant, but when I said we wanted to learn how to speak Yorkshire, he was won over, but only on the understanding that this was to be a secret. And I said it would have to be a secret because Papa and Aunt Branwell would never permit us to play together as they (the Claytons) were from the lower orders and besides there was no chaperone. Aunt Branwell is a terrible snob.

We arranged our meetings in advance, very skilfully; down by the bank of Sladen Beck near the bridge (not far from Forks House where the Claytons lived at one time) there is a curious rock — it has a little hollow in it facing the stream —one can only see it if one kneels down and bends right over. If we plan to meet the next day, we leave a pebble in the hollow, and then, if the other two can come, they also leave a pebble. Then we all check on the morning of the day in question, and if there are two pebbles in the hollow, we know to meet up at the top of the big waterfall on Crow Hill. Everything went surprisingly smoothly. We would meet in the late afternoons, usually on a Friday. Our games became quite complicated, with many characters, but the main players were Augusta (myself) and Juliet (Anne) and their friends, Alexander (Robert) and Roderick (John) and enemies, Gerald (John) and Julius (Robert). As I said, the story takes place on Vision Island at the Palace of Instruction, and our adventures involve either some sort of magical creature or device which we have to find (go on a quest), or fights in which the heroine and her friends defend themselves against the wicked Gerald and his friends. But sometimes we also have rebellions (with much swordplay) against the teachers who are terrible slave-drivers — except for one, an ancient greybeard, who teaches us astronomy, and has the power to revive the dead and foresee the future. (He's a bit like old Mr. Kay, our local astrologer, only much more powerful.) John plays the old man very well — he stoops over and pretends to be blind, and talks in a funny voice, very shaky. Lately we have decided that the four friends will be marooned on a distant island (punishment for a school rebellion) which has never before been explored. I call it Gaaldine.

It took some time to teach the Claytons how to talk like gentry, but they were both good mimics, and eventually could sound just like Aunt Branwell. And we even started to teach them to read, which was hard work but often very comical. But the best part was that the lads knew some wonderful places on the moors where we could play in secret. I like the old quarry the best — it is almost completely hidden, and has great stone platforms at different levels, which are good for dramatic speeches and for battle scenes. They taught us the Yorkshire dialect, and we do pretty well, though I had some trouble with the vowel sounds at first. For instance, suppose one was supposed to say the word, 'sound', it comes out 'sahnd', and 'down' is 'dahn'. That's not exactly right, but it's near. And of course there are whole new words to learn. I've told Tabby what we are doing (she was a bit cross, but promised not to tell Aunt or Papa), and she has helped me and Anne with the new vocabulary. But enough of that.

So things went on like that for quite a long time; we were never caught as we had learned to be very careful. Naturally we four couldn't meet in the wintertime, but in the spring and summer and well into the autumn we managed to play out on the moors about once a week. When Charlotte came home from school in June, last year, we feared we might be forced to give up our games as she became our instructress, but in the end we only had lessons in the morning, and if we finished our chores and the weather was fine, we escaped to freedom in the late afternoon. I think Charlotte was relieved not to be bothered with us. But this spring there was a serious influenza epidemic. That was the beginning of a new era. But I will write about that some other time. Goodnight, little friends.

E.J. Brontë

Those were happy days indeed. After 1835 there was never again that sense of unrestricted freedom, of joy in being young and carefree. And half the pleasure was in keeping it a secret from Papa and Aunt — even Charlotte was not let in on our clandestine romps on the moors with the Claytons, though I think she was suspicious. Branwell, on the other hand, soon found out what was going on from his friends in the village, but we swore him on pain of death to keep quiet. As he was up to various things of which Papa and Aunt would not approve, he agreed to a mutual pact of silence.

I have so many happy memories of our adventures with John and Robert — I can see the four of us now, running along the path above Upper Ponden toward the top of the waterfall, shrieking and laughing. Someone always tripped and fell, and my knees still show the scars of many a tumble. But we never minded; it was all part of that spirit of joyous camaraderie we shared.

I must correct one part of Emily's account of how we met the Claytons, however. She seems to say it was all her own idea; actually it was the Claytons who first approached us. We had been acting out a scene in which Princess Augusta (Emily) was teaching her friend, Lady Juliet (me), to ride a horse, so we were both pretending to be on horseback. This must have looked highly comical as we trotted along, bobbing up and down, holding invisible reins. The Claytons, who were coming down the road toward us, were convulsed with laughter, and demanded to know what was wrong with our legs. It was embarrassing in the extreme, but Emily turned it to our advantage by describing some of the more exciting aspects of our stories. The suggestion that John and Robert join in the games came at our next meeting, I think, but they were clearly captivated from the beginning by Emily's sparkling eyes and lively chatter. I could see that Robert was smitten at once. His normally serious face gradually began to reflect Emily's animated expression, a smile hovering about his lips, and his eyes alight with attention. In fact, it was Robert who later tentatively suggested that he and his brother might perhaps play small parts in our story. Emily immediately saw the advantages and, to Robert's delight, warmly welcomed the idea. Robert was such a good-hearted lad, handsome in a rather rough way, usually quiet and taciturn, kind to animals and children.

John was of a more guarded nature, a bit cynical, and a little cruel. But as our friendship progressed he, too, began to respond to Emily's happy influence.

AB

Great heavens, I had no idea that all this was going on as early as this. And now I understand why Emily and Anne were always so eager to be off over the moors every summer afternoon! Branwell used to drop veiled hints of his own activities (drinking and fisticuffs mainly) — which was easy enough to believe. But it seems quite incredible that Emily and Anne managed to conceal their secret meetings with these young men for several years! Yet how can I blame them; I know full well that both Papa and Aunt would have been scandalized, as indeed they were when they finally found out.

I often think that Aunt, who took her duties as our custodian and task-mistress very seriously, must have resented this enormous burden placed upon her when Mother died. I try to imagine now how she must have felt to leave her comfortable life in Penzance, and be transplanted to cold, unfriendly Yorkshire, and to look after her younger sister's husband and six children! No wonder she sent us off to boarding school at the earliest opportunity. She always did her duty, but there was no love in it, except for Anne, the baby, and Branwell, the darling boy.

CB

To continue my story. So many deaths occurred close to us in the spring of this year that we feared even for ourselves. For Anne and myself the saddest events were the deaths of our friend, John Clayton, and two days later, Sarah Greenwood. I know I haven't spoken before of Sarah, but it is important that you know about her and her family as they are our most important friends in the village. Sarah was the eldest daughter of Joseph Greenwood of Springhead (he is the most important of all the Church Trustees, and a great friend of Papa); she was exactly the same age as Charlotte. We have known the family ever since we came to Haworth. After Mother died more than ten years ago, Sarah's grandmother (Mrs. James Greenwood) was quite concerned about us, so we went to tea at her house (Bridgehouse, at the bottom of the hill) several times. Aunt Branwell went with us of course. Mrs. Greenwood was a great matriarch, very imposing and rather frightening. I remember that Charlotte was rude to Aunt one time while we were there, and Mrs. Greenwood told Charlotte she would never be invited to tea again unless she apologized to Aunt. Charlotte did apologize, but I think she wouldn't have minded not going to tea. After Mrs. Greenwood was widowed in 1824 she didn't invite us any more. She died almost two years ago. In any case, that was how we came to know her three granddaughters, Sarah, Martha, and Anne, and their two brothers, William and James. We visit them often at their fine house, Springhead, which is just down the hill from us at the bottom of Lord Lane, on the other side of the river. Papa and Aunt Branwell think they are the most respectable family in the neighbourhood, even though the middle sister, Martha, is almost an idiot. But Sarah and the youngest girl, Anne (she is exactly the same age as our Anne) are (were) interesting, intelligent girls, so when Sarah died it was a great shock. We have so few friends in the village, that to lose even one is a sad reduction in the stock. And her death has reminded us all of the loss of our own dear sisters 8 years ago. Charlotte and I have painted little portraits of Sarah which we intend to give the family as memorials.

But to return to the death of the friend dearest to Anne and myself — John Clayton. He died in the great influenza epidemic, just like Sarah. After his funeral it was several days before I saw Robert. I had to be very careful because it was still a secret that we were friends. He was very cut up over John's death. It took weeks to cheer him up, but Anne and I did our best to take his mind off his loss. Our games can never be the same now. Anne thinks we should discontinue them, and so we must for the present. John's death has left an enormous gap in our lives. He was always kind to us, and a good friend, and his brother worshipped him. I think I can even find it in my heart to forgive his cruelty in snaring the birds and rabbits. After all, the Clayton family depended on John for much of their daily fare, while we are able to purchase our meat from Mr. Thomas.

Another death about that time which had an effect on our lives was that of Mr. John Greenwood. He was Sarah's uncle (brother of Mr. Joseph), and he and the youngest brother, James, owned and ran Bridgehouse Mill, the largest mill in the town. There was a lot of bad feeling between Mr. Joseph and his brothers, John and James. And when James inherited the whole Greenwood estate (which had been entailed on Mr. Joseph, Sarah's father!!) after John died, things went from bad to worse. In fact, Charlotte even had to postpone a visit from her school friend, Ellen Nussey. Ellen was supposed to visit us early in July, but the town was in an uproar after the reading of John Greenwood's will (he had died at the end of June). Not only did it disinherit Joseph Greenwood and leave everything to James, but it left money to his sister's illegitimate son, Edward, and brought that scandal back into everyone's minds. Papa was very upset and Aunt Branwell thought it would make a very bad impression on Ellen Nussey, whom Papa and Aunt wanted to impress. I was disgusted by the whole affair.

However, Ellen Nussey finally arrived toward the end of July for her long-anticipated visit. I must admit I like her very much. She is rather quiet and a little timid, but she was game for long walks on the moors, and I was impressed by the intelligent way she spoke, and the courage she showed when we were confronted by a herd of cows. Also, she likes Grasper which is always a good omen. Papa and Aunt were very pleased that Charlotte has made such a good (and respectable) friend. I had to smile at Papa's gallant conduct toward her — he was truly charming. Every morning of her visit we would all sit at breakfast listening to his tales of local history and legends, stories we had already heard, but his retelling now gained much in drama and colour. My favourite is the tale of how the Midgleys got their hands on the Manor of Haworth back in the 17th century (on the turn of a card!) and the disgraceful way old Mr. Midgley treated his wife — they say he forced her to submit to barbarous rituals with ropes and chains, and kept her locked in the house all the time, and finally she had enough and threw herself to her death from the attic window. And they say that to this day, her ghost walks in the old part of the Manor House. And then there are all the many tales about the Heatons of Ponden, some of them not so long ago too. And they have their very own ghost — an old man with a beard who appears when one of the Heatons is about to die! Papa can be a wonderful story-teller. But enough of that.

The highlight of Miss Ellen's visit was our great excursion to Bolton Abbey. It is a beautiful and highly romantic place, and we enjoyed ourselves immensely. Well, most of the time. There was a dreadful moment when we first arrived at the Devonshire Arms to meet Ellen's family, and the young lads who handle the horses made very insulting comments on our admittedly rather shabby conveyance and the poor beast drawing it. But then the Nussey family swept up in their elegant carriage and pair, and greeted us most cordially. That put a different complexion on the matter, and after that we were treated with some semblance of respect.

Then in August, Robert and I had a terrifying adventure. We decided to sneak into the grounds of Mr. James Greenwood's new house, Woodlands. This was a daring and dangerous thing to do as Mr. James and Papa weren't on speaking terms (mainly because of the way he had treated his brother Joseph who was Papa's good friend, but also because he is a staunch Baptist, while Mr. Joseph is a Churchman), but we were curious about this new grand house. So early one morning I stole out of the house and met Robert outside the Old Hall, halfway down the hill. Woodlands could be approached from the back through a gate into the stable yard on Stubbings Lane, only a hundred yards from the Old Hall. We climbed over the gate and made our way to the front of the house. It was very quiet, and the dogs appeared to be asleep. Robert held me up so I could look in the window. The room I saw was very large and beautiful; it was all white, with red silk curtains and turkey carpets on the floor. But just as I got down, we heard the dogs wake up. There must have been three of them. Robert just said, 'Run!', and we ran like the wind down the hill across the lawn. But I lost my footing and fell down and then one of the beasts clamped his foul mouth on my left forearm. Robert hit him over the head with his fist, but that didn't work, so he actually pried the creature's jaw open with a stone. I jumped up at once and ran on down to the beck at the bottom of the hill, Robert and the dogs close behind me. We scrambled to the other side of the stream, and luckily the dogs gave up the chase and went back up to the house. My sleeve was all torn and my arm bloody, so Robert helped me bathe the wound, and then wrap it with a strip of my shift. That was the end of our adventure. Robert thought we'd better go home separately before we were seen, so after we regained the main road by Bridgehouse Mill, he went off along the river toward Stanbury, and I climbed the hill to home, all the while trying to think how I was going to explain my wound. I could hardly tell Papa that Robert and I had been trespassing on enemy territory, and been attacked by a guard dog. That would get Robert in trouble, as well as exposing our friendship. It had to be a convincing story and involve only me.

By the time I reached home, I was not only worried about being found out, but also about the risk of hydrophobia. So I went straight into the kitchen where

Tabby was already busy with breakfast, took an iron from the fire, and cauterised the wound. It hurt like blazes and I nearly fainted. Then I had to explain to Tabby what had happened. I told her the whole story, but we agreed I'd better not tell Papa or Aunt the truth. I wanted not to tell them anything at all, but Tabby very wisely said that I should be ready if questioned, so we made up a story about me giving a stray dog a drink of water, and it biting me. That seemed convincing enough, though I wasn't sure Papa would believe I could be so stupid.

But the worst was yet to come. I did have to lie to Papa several days later as the wound, which I had kept concealed in my long sleeve, became horribly swollen and oozing yellow slime. I felt dizzy and sick, and finally fainted. Doctor Andrew was summoned, and he said it was erysipelas, and that I would have to have the infected area cut away. The pain was nearly unbearable and I fainted again. That was nearly two months ago and I am now so thin my bones all show through my skin, and I have a frightful scar on my left arm. Charlotte, Anne, and Branwell were really kind and good to me while I was an invalid. They had written a long story, and read me instalments most evenings before bed. It was called the Green Dwarf, and it starts with Lord Charles convalescing after an illness (like me!) and he is told a long story by Sergeant Bud. Charlotte had already written it before I was ill, which was fortunate indeed. The heroine was called Emily Charlesworth, in my honour. Even Aunt was kind to me, and made special food for me as most normal food made me vomit.

E.J. Brontë

19

Emily told me at that time of her illness that she had a premonition that she would die young. I told her not to be silly, but she was convinced that she would never live to a great age.

AB

I remember Sarah Greenwood's death very clearly (she was such a lovely and intelligent girl), and the influenza epidemic. But I think I must have assumed that Anne and Emily were only grieving over Sarah, though all the while they were also grief-stricken over young John Clayton. I finally was told all about their secret interest in the Clayton boys after Emily's and Robert's adventure at Woodlands, when she confided to me the real cause of the dog bite one evening while she was so ill, and I had been reading to her The Green Dwarf. I think she thought I already knew all about it as I had written of Lady Emily Charlesworth's love for a commoner. But of course, it was only a coincidence. At that time I had no idea how very deep Emily's feelings for Robert were; time was to show us all the profundity of that relationship — Emily changed into a strange and solitary creature after Robert's death, never fully permitting any of us to intrude on her inmost thoughts.

As for the scandal that rocked the village, I am quite sure it started long before we ever heard about it, even before we came to Haworth. Old Mr. Greenwood's daughter Elizabeth had been seduced by her brother-in-law, the great mill-owner in Keighley, William Sugden, and bore a child. That must have been about 1810. After that she was banished to Clitheroe with the baby (Edward). The first I heard of it was in 1825, just after we came home from the school at Cowan Bridge — old Mr. Greenwood had died and left money to the boy and his mother, and we overheard Aunt and Papa talking about it. Tabby told us the details. But it wasn't until the death of Mary Ann Sugden, (William Sugden's wife and daughter of Mr. Greenwood) in 1832, that the rumours of a curse began to circulate and then in 1834 her wicked husband also died leaving Edward, his bastard son, a thousand pounds! It was the gossip of all Keighley and Haworth, and I must confess that these events made a deep impression on me. The Greenwoods were a proud and cruel family, generous with their wealth, but unkind and unforgiving toward their children.

CB

It has been several years now since I wrote down the events of my life. So much has happened, I find it difficult to remember everything. And there are some events I would prefer to forget. However, I will try to leave nothing important out, no matter how painful. I fear my little imaginary readers have all vanished into air, and now I write only for myself. Some day I may wish to remember all this.

The year 1834 was on the whole a good year. The great event for me was the acquisition of our own piano. We all learned to play a little, having lessons at home from Mr. Sunderland who came over from Keighley once a week. Charlotte gave up almost at once (she is so short-sighted she couldn't see the music), but Anne, Branwell, and I became quite proficient, and Anne and I can play many duets. But I am the only one who really enjoys practising and playing for my own amusement, especially now... Branwell prefers the new organ in the church because he likes the sense of power it gives him. He also likes the flute; he says at least he can carry it about with him.

Both Charlotte and Branwell are enthusiastic artists — Branwell does portraits in oils (making us sit for him for hours), and Charlotte copies from engravings. She is very good at it (she had two pictures in a big exhibition in Leeds), but I think she will never be an original artist as her eyesight is so bad, she can't see clearly the objects she wants to draw. I myself have done several sketches and water colours from life, which I enjoy, but I prefer music to all other artistic pursuits.

And of course, Charlotte and Branwell continued to be obsessed with their secret writing. Papa discovered some of their tiny manuscripts and became suspicious, and insisted that Charlotte write large and legibly. So she wrote some rather tame poems into her new exercise book for Papa to find, though all the while she was secretly writing the most scandalous stories. After that, of course, she was very careful to conceal her papers.

In November of 1834 Anne and I decided to write a private paper describing a particular day. We picked the

24th of the month, a Monday. It would not be at all like this Journal which is only mine and very personal — it would be much more about the very day it was written, so we could read it some years later and truly remember what it was like to be us on that day. Of course, I didn't mention the Claytons — at that time our friendship was still a secret from Papa and Aunt.

1835 opened on a sad note — our dear sexton, William Brown, died. He had been such a support to Papa over the years, and we had known him nearly all our lives. His post was taken on by his son, John, who is a jolly man whom we all like very much. He and Branwell are thick as thieves, and they have a plan to enable B to join the Three Graces Lodge as soon as possible. Aunt, naturally, is very sceptical that this is a wise course.

Now I must write something terribly personal, but as it is an important event in the life of any young girl, it must be recorded: earlier in the year (February, I think) I awoke one morning with an acute pain in my belly, and when I left my bed I felt a warm trickle running down my leg. I looked to see what it was and was shocked to see it was blood! And there were spots of blood on my nightdress and on the sheet. I think I screamed. By this time Anne and Charlotte were both standing about like frightened rabbits, their faces registering nothing useful. So I shouted for Tabby to come help me. She came puffing up the stairs, genuinely alarmed, but when she saw the problem, she only laughed, and informed me — 'Eh, lass, tha' hast becum a womun na'.' But she wouldn't explain to me what she meant. At this point Aunt, hearing us all talking at once, entered the room. She knew immediately what to do — she told Tabby to find some old bed linen and cut it up to make several napkins, and she told me how to wear them. 'Of course, you will have to hem the edges very carefully as they will be frequently laundered', she informed me. That was all very well, but by evening the pain was excruciating, and Papa decided that Mr. Andrew must be summoned first thing in the morning. I protested in vain and begged Papa simply to follow the

23

advice in Graham's book.* The memory of the previous autumn's ghastly operation on my arm, which Mr. Andrew performed with a certain amount of gusto, had left me very sceptical about his sympathy for his patient's feelings, and I certainly did not want him inspecting my nether regions with his great spidery hands. But Papa brooked no contradiction, and the man was duly sent for. Oh, I hope I never have to see another doctor again! After poking and prodding my body and talking to Aunt as if I weren't even present, he concluded that the pain was perfectly normal, and suggested warm baths to 'encourage the flow', and, then, just before he departed he advised Aunt to explain to me the significance of what was happening. This was very important, he said, as I was now sufficiently mature to conceive a child! And he left, without even suggesting a physic for the pain! Aunt was quite overcome with embarrassment, and had no idea how to explain exactly how one conceives a baby. However, I had a pretty good idea already, for various reasons, so I simply described to her what I knew, and she blushed and confirmed my observations. I think I probably know more about these things than she does, mainly because Branwell explained a lot of things to me not long before. Aunt was always telling us about her lively girlhood in Penzance, and how many admirers she had, but in truth she seems to know very little about the ways of the male sex. No wonder she's an old maid!

I passed on to Charlotte and Anne a full description of what had transpired. Charlotte felt a bit cross that I was the first of us to reach this milestone; she thought she should have been the first entitled to the dubious distinction of menstruation, seeing as she is the eldest. As to the rest of it, she was silent and thoughtful. Anne, however, simply didn't believe it — 'Oh, that is absolutely disgusting — no woman would submit to such a violation! That can't be true!' But we have all seen sheep and dogs doing it, so she knows it must be true.

* Our excellent family medical book is Modern Domestic Medicine, by Thomas John Graham, M.D. and is consulted and annotated by Papa in conjunction with the advice of a doctor or surgeon. Ed.

The next event in my life will, I think, be remembered by me until I die — I hope I can write it sensibly. Needless to say, after John Clayton's death, I spent a great deal of my free time with Robert, frequently without Anne, who was often too busy with sewing to come away. Robert and I had always been great friends, but by the summer of 1834 somehow our friendship seemed to have changed and deepened. For example, whenever we planned to meet, and Anne was for some reason not able to join us, I experienced strange feelings of excitement and nervousness in anticipation, but when we were together these feelings were replaced by ones of almost magical elation. And the games we played, when it was only the two of us, became more and more romantic. Looking back, it is starkly clear where things were headed.

To cut my story short, the inevitable finally happened in the late spring of the following year (that's 1835). Indeed, two inevitable events occurred. We were in our secret quarry, working out a new scene in which Augusta is searching the battlefield for her lover, Alexander Elbë, who has been wounded (though the Royalist forces have been victorious) and may be dying. But just as I approached the rock on which Alexander (Robert) was reclining, I slipped on the wet moss, and fell heavily against him. Suddenly he put his arms around me and kissed me. I was quite swept away. I wanted that moment to last forever. I remember thinking, I will never in my whole life to come be happier than I am at this moment. And we just sat there, holding each other, sometimes kissing, sometimes talking quietly. It seemed almost as if we had become one person.

This is very hard to write. A short while later we heard a smothered cry from the entrance to the quarry. A little boy was standing there, his mouth hanging open. We both leapt up instantly; I couldn't believe what was happening. To go from heaven into hell in one second!

Of course, that was the beginning of the end. Robert recognized the boy as Nathan, the son of Bill Shackleton of Rush Isles. He had been out on the moor looking for stray ewes and lambs. Young Nathan ran away as fast as his little legs could carry him, and we were sure he would tell his father and mother, who would then tell Mrs. Heaton, who would then tell Aunt Branwell. And that is exactly what happened.

Papa and Aunt were apoplectic with fury. It seems Mrs. Heaton had cornered Aunt after morning service the very next Sunday and expressed her shock and dismay that the Parson's daughter should be consorting with the likes of Robert Clayton, a mere weaver's son. She knew just the right words to inflame Aunt's sense of class transgression.

That afternoon Aunt confronted me with the accusation. I was unprepared for the swiftness of the attack, and could only acknowledge the truth of the story, but then, there would have been little point in denying anything. And it would have been deeply disloyal to Robert, who, I was sure, was already being punished. Of course I expected severe punishment myself. But I never expected the radical extremes to which Papa and Aunt were prepared to go.

The following day Papa called me into his study after breakfast (which had been a silent meal, even Branwell held his peace) and I stood before him, my heart sinking and my stomach churning. I was informed that not only was I never to see Robert again, but that I was to be sent away to school as soon as it could be arranged. Papa refused to hear anything I might say in my defence. I have never seen him so angry.

That was in June; by July they had arranged everything. Because Branwell hoped to go up to London and the Royal Academy Schools, Charlotte had volunteered to take on a teaching post at Roe Head to pay my school fees — money was as usual in very short supply. In the end Branwell didn't go to London — it seems that it was more important to tear me away from everything and everyone I loved than to give the only Brontë son a good preparation for his career. I can still feel the anger seething in the pit of my being when I think about the cruelty and injustice of this. Anne says I am being silly to hold this grudge, and that Branwell was persuaded by Mr. Robinson, his teacher in Leeds, that he was not ready for the R.A. yet, and needed to perfect and enlarge his portfolio, and so it had nothing to do with my school fees. Well, perhaps, but I think Papa was determined to send me away, and actively discouraged Branwell from going up to London.

Both Anne and Charlotte tried to be understanding, but how could I explain to them the depth of despair into which I was plunged. To be banished from home was bad enough, but to be separated from Robert just when we realized how much we loved each other was insupportable.

Finally the day came on which Charlotte and I left for Roe Head. It was the day before my 17th birthday. How I survived the next two months I hardly know. At first I was unable to eat or sleep, and I cried almost continually. By the end of the first month I realized that I was growing very thin, and it occurred to me in my semi-crazed state of mind that if I stopped eating altogether, I would either die, or they would send me home. Either alternative seemed equally desirable. Also, my monthly bleeding stopped, which convinced Charlotte that I was in a serious condition. Finally she took matters into her own hands and spoke to Mrs. Franks and the headmistress, Miss Wooler, assuring them that I was on the point of death. I never knew whether it was Miss Wooler or Mrs. Franks who finally wrote to Papa, but at last my recall was successfully obtained in mid-October.

But at home things have been only slightly better. Though I eat the food put before me, sleeping is very difficult. It was over a month before I was well enough even to help Tabby in the kitchen. I don't know what I would do without Tabby. As Anne was immediately sent to Roe Head in my place, Tabby is now my only friend in the house, besides Grasper, of course. Sometimes Branwell is sympathetic, but he is often away in Leeds or immersed in his endless History of Angria. Papa and Aunt still treat me as a rebellious and wicked child, but Tabby is always there to smooth my ruffled feathers, and to her I can talk about Robert, which is a relief. She had known the Clayton family in the old days before she came to work for us and thought highly of Robert's parents. The Claytons are among the last of the Stanbury Quaker community, and they were once a successful and respected yeoman family, but they have come

27

on hard times since the War, like so many others.

My punishment continues. If the weather permits, which has been rare this winter, I am allowed to walk out if accompanied by Branwell or Tabby, but only as far as Oxenhope or Stanbury, and we must stay on the main road. Branwell is good company, but we rarely talk about what has happened, and we generally discuss what he is writing, or books and articles we've read, or about people in the village. I am not allowed to speak or write to anyone outside the immediate family. Aunt has made certain that I never have an unoccupied moment, and that I am rarely alone before bedtime. I practice the piano incessantly (music is the great comforter), whenever I have finished the mountain of chores heaped upon me. This usually consists of sewing for Anne and Charlotte. One day is identical to the others, grey and dreary. I am miserable.

Anne has already written me several letters since she left. They are often rather short but nonetheless very welcome. I'm sure poor Anne is herself enduring a great ordeal; she is so inexperienced in the way of life in a proper school, and she is also very homesick. I have written to her three times already, but this may only make matters worse as my letters are a constant reminder that we are separated. I enclose the first of her dear letters in the pages of this journal. The letter was evidently written under Miss Wooler's watchful eye. I only hope she doesn't read the letters which I send to Anne!

I must conclude this account of my life which is now brought up to date.

E.J. Brontë

_____

(Anne's letter)

Dearest Em,

I take this opportunity to write to you my one weekly letter. Miss Wooler has kindly suggested that a letter to you would be most beneficial to both of us, separated as we now are and as we have never been before. She says she does not fully understand what drove you to such an extreme demonstration of unhappiness, but she is willing to accept my word that I at least am in full possession of the facts, and she does not expect me to reveal them.

My life here is not intolerable. The other girls are friendly and very lively, and although I have not yet made any close friends, I find the peace and orderliness of the daily routine very soothing. Also our school work is much less demanding than I feared. That said, I miss you dreadfully, and also Tabby and Branwell. I rarely see Charlotte in private. We have spoken briefly on two occasions, and that only to exchange letters from home. She is finding her work very hard. If only she were a little older, it would be easier for her, but because she is only a few years older than the oldest pupils, and also because she is so much smaller than they, she is finding it hard to keep discipline even with the younger ones.

Write to me soon, and tell me all the news. Send my love to Aunt and Papa, and tell Tabby I miss her very much. And tell Branwell to behave himself and to go walking with you whenever you desire it.

love from your devoted though distant sister,

Anne

—————————————

29

I remember the day Emily came home from Roe Head so clearly; it was a time laden with many different emotions and all I could do was hug her bony form and weep. She really was very ill. Though I dreaded the thought of leaving her and setting off for Roe Head the next day, I was so glad she was home again.

As it turned out, school was not the great trial for me that it had been for Emily, at least not at first; I even made a good friend eventually. But she died a few years later, and I have never had another close female friend since, except for Emily, and even we were never as close after I went away to school. How I envy Charlotte her long friendship with Ellen Nussey and Mary Taylor. Surely friendship is one of the greatest boons that life can bestow. I have never felt so alone.

AB

———————————

I refrained from commenting on this entry in the Journal, or on Anne's pathetic note while she yet lived. The guilt I feel over Anne's loneliness when I could have helped her and been a better friend to her torments me still. My only explanation for my selfishness is that she and I had never been 'friends' as children, and I always saw her as the baby of the family while I was burdened with all the responsibilities expected of the eldest child. And both Papa and Aunt petted and spoiled her, so perhaps I was resentful. But at Roe Head I was so consumed with anxiety over my duties that I barely noticed her existence until she too became ill. Then I went too far and blamed Miss Wooler for being callous to Anne's condition, when, of course, I now realize it was I who had been callous. And then after Emily died, I was cast into the pit of despair, and because Anne was so silent in her suffering and grief, I paid insufficient attention to her mental anguish. Often I even felt angry that she was ill — how dare she be ill when I had just lost the person dearest to me in the world! Well, it is too late now to make amends. 'Hollows Mill' will have to be my only apology; Caroline Helstone has many of Anne's characteristics, and I have given her a mother to bring her back to life and to love her.*

One last comment on matters of fact: Emily's recall from Roe Head was obtained by me, but only after I enlisted the help of dear Mrs. Franks. She told me that Papa had already written

---

* *Hollow's Mill* was my original title for *Shirley,* it was changed shortly after I wrote the above comments. Ed.

her a warning letter[*] in July (of which we had no knowledge at the time) that Emily might cause trouble, so when Mrs. F., who therefore visited us frequently at school (she came every few weeks), saw for herself that Emily was failing in health, I persuaded her to intervene with Miss Wooler, and they agreed that if there were no improvement in the next few weeks, Emily should be sent home. She also wrote to Papa to this effect, and permission was granted, thank God. Emily was at home before the end of October.

Papa was more inclined to be sympathetic than Aunt, but he was very concerned about Emily's 'moral character'. And indeed he had much to lose if there were a scandal in the family — his (and our) very livelihood depended upon it. Yet I think his anxiety was also caused partly by his fear that, having, by his own efforts, lifted himself out of the ranks of the poor Irish working classes, and become a university-educated gentleman and a respected clergyman, a disgrace in the family would lead to an inexorable regression into the shameful poverty he had worked so diligently to leave behind.

C Brontë

---

[*] Mrs. Franks later allowed me transcribe the letter my father had sent to her that July of 1835; it contained the following words of warning: "As two of my dear children are soon to be placed near you, I take the liberty of writing to you a few lines in order to request both you and Mr. Franks to be so kind as to interpose with your advice and counsel to them in any case of necessity, and, if expedient, to write to Miss Branwell or me if our interference should be requisite. I will charge them strictly to attend to what you may advise, though it is not my intention to speak to them of this letter. They both have good abilities, and as far as I can judge their principles are good also, but they are very young, and unacquainted with the ways of this delusive and insnaring world; and though they will be placed under the superintendence of Miss Wooler, who will I doubt not do what she can for their good, yet I am well aware that neither they not any other can ever, in this land of probation, be beyond the reach of temptation." The thinly veiled concern which Papa felt for Emily is clearly evident, and Mrs. Franks was in no doubt that his letter referred only to her. They certainly had no worries on my account. Ed.

It has been over a year now since I last wrote the events of my life. My life has entirely changed. Grief and guilt have been my constant companions, and when I am able to sleep, I dream dreams so fearful that waking is, momentarily, a relief. Then I lie awake, hours before sunrise, the events of the last year swirling about me like ghosts.

Here is an account of the significant events of the year 1836.

In the spring of the year, Aunt Branwell's attitude toward me changed. She had been cold and critical, and I in turn had faced her condemnation with sullen, silent obedience. But then in April, for reasons I soon learned, she took a different approach. At breakfast one morning she gaily announced to me and Branwell that we had been invited to a party, and she actually encouraged me to attend. I was very reluctant at first, until I realized that this might be a safe opportunity to learn something of Robert, whom I had not seen or heard from for almost a year. And so I agreed, which pleased Papa and Aunt greatly.

The party was to be given by the Greenwoods of Spring Head on the following Friday evening — there was to be music and dancing. Aunt was in her element deciding what I should wear, even making the necessary alterations herself to my one good dress (grey silk) so that it looked more suitable for an evening party. She insisted on lending me her coral beads and best shawl. I was rather puzzled by her concern over my appearance — she had never bothered before — but I should have realized at once that she had plans for me of which I was meant to know nothing.

The evening of the party was cool and damp but not actually raining. Branwell and I trotted off down the hill, he full of good cheer and jollity, I feeling foolish and self-conscious, with Aunt's words ringing in my head — to stand up straight, keep my shawl over my scarred left arm, and not to refuse every dance. Never have I so fervently wished that I were three inches shorter. Anne Greenwood welcomed us at the door and ushered us into the elegant drawing room.

The musicians were already in place, and most of the guests had arrived. The carpet was rolled back, and dancing was about to commence. Branwell joined a group of his friends at once, and Anne went to greet some newcomers (the Merrall boys), so I was left standing alone in a corner, wishing I had never come. Of course I knew who most of the guests were, but no one well enough to approach directly. But soon Anne returned bringing her brother James with her. Although I have known James all my life, this was the first time I had ever seen him so elegantly dressed; he looked quite grown-up. And finally I understood Aunt's plan: Papa, Aunt, and Mr. Greenwood, with his daughter's help, were conspiring to match me with James Greenwood. It was all an elaborate scheme to take my mind off Robert. Aunt must have suggested this plan to Papa, who spoke of it to Mr. Joseph Greenwood, and with his help and that of his daughter, they arranged this party, and plotted to make sure I spent most of my time with James. Indeed it was not long after this that I realized they even meant (well, hoped) to marry me off to such a respectable suitor. And most 'respectable' James is: his father is not only the Lord of the Manor of Oxenhope, but also the first magistrate in this locality — a marriage to one of his sons would mean a great step upward on the social ladder hereabouts — Papa and Aunt would be highly gratified. I wonder whether James was aware of the plot at that time, and whether the Greenwoods knew about Robert.

And now I must admit that my second reaction was one of pleasure. I was thankful that it was James and not his brother William who was to be the lamb to the slaughter. William is coarse, fat, stupid, and overbearing, without a trace of sentiment or tenderness. At least James is kind and well-read, and very attractive in a rather girlish way. He has fine light brown hair, serious grey-blue eyes, and his figure is slender and well-proportioned.

I felt so sorry for him, as he stood there, speechless and blushing with embarrassment. So I took pity and asked if he would show me the new library. He brightened considerably at this, and we spent the next hour looking over Mr. Greenwood's fine collection of books and prints. James is remarkably intelligent, and the time passed agreeably. Perhaps I encouraged him too much, however. At the end of the evening, after the supper and more dancing (I did dance one dance with James, a waltz), he asked if he could call. And of course I said I would have to ask Aunt, but that I would send him a note.

That was the beginning of our 'courtship'. All through the summer we walked out together, though never on the moors. There were visits to his cousins in Heptonstall and Utley, tea parties, dances, even riding, which I took to very quickly. Usually his sister went with us, and sometimes Aunt. We were never alone together, not even on horseback; then either his father or brother rode with us. It was all very light-hearted, on my part at least. But by the end of the summer I began to weary of being a respectable young lady, and longed to be away from the suffocating conventions of what was 'proper' and 'correct'.

In the meantime I hadn't forgotten Robert. With the coming of fine weather and long days in June, I stole out of the house very early one morning and made my way out to Robert's home at Far Slack, hoping to find him. I remember it was a beautiful morning, and to walk alone at last over the vast moorland through the morning mists, all golden in the rising sun, was pure pleasure. When I arrived at Far Slack it was quickly apparent that no one was stirring yet, so I walked onward to one of our old trysting places, the secret quarry. Then, to my amazement, I saw Robert coming down the path toward me! We flew to each other. When we had caught our breath, we both began talking at once — I saying how much I had missed him, but was being kept a virtual prisoner, and he saying that he came by the Parsonage nearly every day trying to catch a glimpse of me. Robert was looking very thin and much older than last summer. I promised him faithfully that I would sneak away at every opportunity, but it was very difficult now. And Charlotte and Anne would soon be home from school which would make it even harder. I never mentioned anything about James Greenwood, and neither did he, so I guessed he didn't know I was 'walking out' with him. At this point I had begun to realize that I was being groomed for marriage, but still I didn't see why I could not be friends with both of them. I felt as if I were two people — one was young and flighty, enjoying being admired and petted — the other was strong and free and loving.

We talked for a while and kissed and embraced, but I soon realized I would have to get back before I was missed. It was hard to leave, but I finally pulled myself away, promising to return as soon as I could. But by the time I finally reached home, I could see by the smoke from the chimney that Tabby was already up and about. I entered the kitchen very quietly, hoping she wouldn't hear me, but the Fates were determined to give me away, and I accidentally nudged a bucket with my foot. Not only was Tabby in the kitchen but Papa as well. He took one look at my muddy boots, and the bits of dried heather on my skirt and hair, and knew exactly where I had been, and, perhaps, what I had been doing. So my doom was sealed. He decreed I was to go to my room and not emerge for a full week; my meals would be brought to me on a tray, and after the week, I was still forbidden to leave the house except to walk in the garden. I gasped. Charlotte and Anne would soon be home — what would they think? And in any case, how could I be kept in my room — where would they sleep? But this is what happened: I was a prisoner for that full week, and my sisters did not return home when expected. By the time they did, at least I could come down for meals. Later I found out how Papa managed this: he discovered (or had he suggested it?) that Mr. and Mrs. Franks had invited Charlotte and Anne to spend a whole week with them before returning home, even though Mrs. Franks was not well. Charlotte wrote to Mrs. Franks requesting that they visit for only a few days, but Papa heard about this and countermanded her request — he insisted they stay for the full week. All this because he refused to commute my sentence.

Of course later I told Anne and Charlotte exactly what had happened. Anne said I was playing with fire, but she understood how I felt. Charlotte was strangely impressed, and said she wished she had the courage to disobey orders

36

and not forever be trying to please everyone.

After that I really didn't dare to try it again. In fact, with James demanding my company at every opportunity, and Aunt watching me like a hawk, it was only in September that I contrived to get away again, and that was because of the urgency of the matter. This is what happened: In September, everything came to a head. First, James asked Papa for 'my hand'. Of course Papa and Aunt were delighted. Aunt even began to make plans for the wedding — where should the dress be made, what would I need for my trousseau, and so on. They both seemed completely unaware that James had not yet asked me, nor had I given an answer. They were quite taken aback when I said I would have to think about it, and would have to talk to James. I had no idea he was so serious. No doubt that was foolish of me. Looking back I could see clearly that he must have taken my delight in our outings together, and my genuine fondness for him, for something much more than friendship. But I did not truly love him, and I knew I had to see Robert before I gave James an answer.

So one day when the usual weekly invitation to tea at Spring Head arrived, I made up my mind to take advantage of this opportunity to see Robert. I would dress myself for the tea party, but I would not attend. Instead I would seek out Robert whom I had not seen since the ill-fated meeting in June — I feared he would think I had betrayed him. Perhaps he had turned his back on our love, even found someone else. Well, if that were the case, then perhaps I would marry James. Although such a marriage would never be ideal, it might develop into a comfortable and pleasant partnership. And heaven knows Aunt and Papa would be mightily relieved to deliver me into the arms of the Greenwood family. At least that is what I thought at that time.

And now I must end this account for the moment. The events which followed were so strange and terrible, that I can write no more tonight.

E. J. Brontë

That summer of 1836 was truly extraordinary. When we came home from Roe Head in June (after our week with the Franks), Emily behaved very strangely. She told me about the meeting with Robert, and about her incarceration (about which she was pretty angry), but then she would go on and on about what a fine fellow James Greenwood was. So I didn't know what she was actually feeling; for the first time she seemed a stranger to me. And it made me very apprehensive for the future.

There were many social events that included all of us, and Aunt and Papa were thrilled at the prospect of Emily 'getting on' with her life — they thought that she had 'got over' Robert, and that she would almost certainly marry young James Greenwood. Aunt was cheerful and excited for the first time in many years.

AB

When Emily told us about her escape from the house and her secret meeting with Robert, I must admit I found myself admiring her daring. She was quite correct; I would love to be brave and daring, throwing caution to the winds and never mind the consequences! But I fear my nature is naturally repressed and timid. I may feel mutinous in my heart, but I suppress my feelings of rage against injustice, and try to meet adversity with a calm exterior, even when I am boiling with anger. My great desire is to be liked and trusted. Emily was never like that. She had the most wonderful ability to be simply herself of anyone I have ever known.

CB

Since I wrote in this journal last month, I have begun to write a few poor lines of verse, hoping that the effort will help me rise from the pit, the abyss, in which I find myself. And in those few moments when the words come quickly and surely, I do find I am lifted out of myself. But when I struggle to find the right word to fit both the metre, rhyme, and the sense, and fail, as so often happens, I throw down my pen, take up my shawl, and summon Grasper for a run on the moors. Papa and Aunt no longer watch me; there is no need any more. I miss Anne terribly and wish she were here.

But to continue my story. On the day I decided to absent myself from the Greenwood tea party, I dressed with unusual care. I remember Aunt even commented on how well I looked, and smiled approvingly as I took my leave. For several weeks she had refrained from accompanying me, no doubt thinking that it was time that James and I spent more time alone together. So I took the accustomed route through the graveyard, past the Church until I was out of sight of the Parsonage. Then I doubled back along West Lane, and cut up the hill to the footpath. I kept to the path as well as I could, trying to avoid being seen by anyone, and finally reached Far Slack. On my arrival Robert, who had been working in the field nearby, called to me. We approached each other slowly, neither of us sure of the other's feelings. He was filthy with mud, and I fear my first reaction was one of distaste. He noticed, of course, and I felt the pain on his face like a sharp knife in my heart. Before I could assure him that my feelings for him were unchanged, he blurted out a reproach so justified that I was momentarily speechless. Was I grown so fine that I no longer wanted to see my old friend? And what was all this talk in the village that I was about to marry 'that mucky rich milksop, James Greenwood'. I was stung by this accusation, and sprang to James' defence — just because James is cultured and gentlemanly is no reason to call him a milksop. At this Robert scowled and was on the point of turning away. But I overcame my revulsion and went to him, and with my hand on his arm, I told him that whether or not I married James was up to himself. Did he still love me? Then he looked at me very searchingly, at my pretty dress and my ringletted hair. "I don't know who you are any more, Em," he said. "If you love me, you'll come away with me, and we'll be wed. If you don't then go and marry Master Greenwood and be damned." Well, this was a great shock to me. The thought of marrying Robert had never entered my head. My silence seemed to speak for me. He looked at me sadly, shook his head, and finally said, "Well then, Em, I suppose that's as good an answer as any." Then he turned and walked back to the house.

I returned home, feeling stunned and confused. Fortunately both Papa and Aunt were away — having tea with the Taylors out in Stanbury, I think. I quickly changed out of my good dress (after removing the mud streaks from the hem), and went to find Tabby. I told her what had transpired, but this time she was not at all sympathetic. In fact, she was quite angry, saying that I had deceived my father and Aunt, and would pay a heavy price for doing so. I begged her not to tell them, and finally convinced her that no good could come of it. She reluctantly agreed, but only because I promised never to do it again, and I think she saw that I was in real distress. Then I went to my room, and tried to think. But it was useless, my mind was quite unable to deal with everything. It all seemed so sudden. And the only thing I was sure of was that I wasn't ready to marry anybody.

For the next few weeks, I struggled with these new thoughts and feelings, but no course of action presented itself. And in the meantime, James finally proposed to me in person, which only made matters worse. I put him off as kindly as possible, much to Aunt's disappointment and disapproval. Tabby and I discussed my dilemma at length, but she refused to tell me what to do. Finally, late in October, I thought that at least I could write to Robert and explain how I felt. Branwell, to my surprise, volunteered to convey the note to Far Slack for me.

Weeks passed. Finally an answer arrived, delivered by young Bob Heaton who was a good friend of Robert. Bob thinks I am some sort of tragic heroine now, and is constantly sending me little presents. He is very sweet. The letter from Robert was intercepted for me by Tabby. I quote at length:

'Deer Em

I got thy note and am sory to take so long to anser. I can not tell thee what to do, but I gess you dont love me, at leest not enuff to come with me. Me and the family are soon moving to a place ner Denholme as my mother is worryd about all the talk about us in the village and my father thinks he will find cole better there, so we are going there soon. Wen I heer that you have wed Mr. James, I will know that thy feelings for me were not enuff. I will love thee allways.

Robert'

I have the note still; it tears at my heart.

In December, just before Anne and Charlotte were to come home for the Christmas holidays, I had a long talk late one night with Tabby. Though she never said in so many words that I shouldn't marry James, she questioned me closely on my feelings for him, and it became very clear that she thought they were not the feelings of someone who had the right reasons to accept a proposal of marriage. On the other hand, she didn't say I should marry Robert. In fact, I think she was truly afraid of what would happen to us as we would be so poor, and that his family would never accept me. I tried to imagine what it would be like living with that very large, hardworking family, which I would have to do as Robert and I have no money of our own. It would be very unpleasant, I think. And of course there would be no possibility of him living here at the Parsonage. These were things I had never thought about. Still, she did say that perhaps Robert might some day make his way in the world (as Papa did) and be able to provide a decent life for us. Some day. So toward midnight, after Tabby had gone up to bed, I decided to write a letter to each of them (James and

41

Robert). I would tell James that I couldn't accept him, and that I was quite the wrong girl for him, although I hoped we could still be friends. Then I would tell Robert how much I loved him, and that if he could earn success in the world, I was prepared to wait for him. For ever, if need be. After that, I felt so alive and hopeful that I wrote a very jolly poem.* It was nearly 3 in the morning by the time I fell asleep.

And now came the worst day of my life. I arose late, and by the time I came down for breakfast, Aunt, Papa, and Branwell were already at table. They all looked at me strangely and were very silent. After breakfast Papa took me into his study. His face was very serious and I felt afraid I was about to be punished again. I thought they must have found out that I had not had tea that day at Spring Head. But no, it was much worse. He had just been asked the day before if he would conduct a funeral service the next afternoon. I can hardly bear to write this. The body to be interred was Robert. My Robert.

I can write no more.

EJB

---

* The poem referred to is dated 13 December, 1836. It is a very unusual poem, unique in Emily's oeuvre, in that it contains no complete sentences, and is simply a joyous evocation of nature. The first verse is:

High waving heather, 'neath stormy blasts bending
Midnight and moonlight and bright shining stars;
Darkness and glory rejoicingly blending,
Earth rising to heaven and heaven descending,
Man's spirit away from its drear dungeon sending,
Bursting the fetters and breaking the bars.

Although she later wrote many poems on the grandeur of nature, none of them evoke so vividly her exuberant oneness with the Universe. Ed.

This entry was a revelation to me. Charlotte and I had been away at school from the end of July, so the events of that autumn were unknown to me; Emily wrote me no letters at all, and I was anxious for her, I felt something was amiss. And when we came home in December, Emily was unable to speak about it. Now at last I truly understand how and why she wrote that painful passage in Wuthering Heights in which Heathcliff is crushed and humiliated by Catherine's behaviour when she returns from Thrushcross Grange. What a burden of guilt she must have carried from that time on.

AB

I fear all I can remember of that time was my eagerness to be at home again after a particularly taxing term of teaching, and to see my great friend Ellen, — and then my anger and disappointment at being swept up in the tragedies of December, all my plans in ruins. I think I was slightly insane for a time.

CB

Since my last entry in this journal I think I have begun to recover a little from the torment which followed Robert's death. Now I go over and over that ghastly time before Christmas, trying to piece together in my mind a clearer picture of all that happened. But whole days are lost now beyond recall. Nevertheless, I will try to reconstitute as best I can the sequence of events beginning with the intelligence of Robert's funeral conveyed to me that morning of the 13th of December by Papa.

My first reaction was one of disbelief. I rushed from the room, convinced that they (Papa and Aunt) were trying to shock me into forgetting about him. I thought they had learned of my secret visit, and were afraid I might run off with him. This was, of course, madness on my part. I sought out John Brown, our sexton, but he confirmed that Papa had only told me the simple fact of the case. After that I shut myself in my room. The days that followed are a blur. I know I heard Charlotte and Anne returning from Roe Head sometime that afternoon. I know that I must have stayed shut up in my room for about three days. The funeral came and went without leaving a trace on my memory. Did I attend? I cannot say. I was later told that I appeared at the door of the church, looking like a spectre, and then disappeared, but I have no recollection of this. But I do remember going out late one evening to find Robert's grave. I suppose it was the same day as the funeral. It was very cold and dark, and I remember thinking that I was going mad and ought to die, even hoping I might freeze to death then and there. Suddenly I heard Tabby calling to me in the graveyard, but then she gave a little shriek. At first I paid no attention, but a little later on I heard someone else say, "Look, it's Mrs. Ackroyd... she's hurt. Go get help, Isaac. Mrs. Hardaker will know what to do. And then tell the Parson." That brought me to my senses. I ran to them, and helped the men carry Tabby to the apothecary. She was in great pain, her leg was bloody and broken. Mrs. Hardaker gave her some laudanum, but could do nothing more until a doctor could be called. It was very late by now, so I sat with her until the morning. During the night Papa had been informed, but it was decided not to risk moving her until Dr. Andrew had seen her leg. He came at last and set the bone as best he could. Then we had to decide what to do next. Of course Aunt wanted Tabby to be moved to her sister's house, but I was adamant. They were all a little afraid of me, I think, and when I said I would stop eating if she weren't to be nursed at the Parsonage, she and Papa gave way. Anne, Charlotte, and Branwell all agreed with me. But poor Charlotte. She had so looked forward to these holidays and now between me and Tabby, her plans were in ruins.

There is not much more to tell. How Robert met his death is still not clear to me. Joe Clayton (Robert's younger brother) told Bob Heaton (who told me) that he had fallen in a bog when working on Black Moor, and had died of the cold before he was found. And it is true that Robert was less familiar with that moor than either Haworth or Stanbury moor, but it is hard to believe that he could have been so careless... O God, I wish I had never sent him that letter! I am tormented by the ghastly fear that he chose to die and that I am responsible.

As for poor James Greenwood, I did turn down his proposal, though I think that my behaviour after Robert's death has probably convinced the Greenwoods that they have had a lucky escape. But James was very hurt and humiliated, and I am very sorry for that; he is a good-hearted fellow, a true 'gentle-man'. I hope he will find someone else.

Now this is the end of my journal. There is no need to write more as I am perfectly confident that life holds nothing more to interest me.

Emily Jane Brontë

(the following letter was inserted here, along with a lock of Anne's hair, now missing)

Dearest Em,

I wish you would write. When I left home last month, you promised faithfully that you would, but I have had nothing from you since. My anxiety about your health grows daily. Please please send word that you are beginning to recover from the terrible events of last December. And tell me what is happening at home — how is Tabby? Is she still bed-ridden? What news of Branwell? I hope he is being a good brother and a friend to you. I know Aunt will take some time to come 'round, but try not to antagonize her. You know she did what she thought was for the best. And Papa I'm sure still loves you dearly, even though he may not show it just now. Does he still have contact with the Greenwoods? Does Charlotte ever write to you? I hardly ever see her, except in the classroom. Please write to me very soon.

Your most loving sister,
Anne

PS I enclose a lock of my hair, and beg you to send me one of yours.

I will never forget that Christmas. Emily — almost deranged with grief and guilt. Charlotte — seething with disappointment, and torn to pieces by her effort to be kind to Emily, nurse Tabby, calm Papa and Aunt, keep the house running, all at the same time. Her escape was to join Branwell — the two of them were submerged in their obsessive chronicles of Angria. They both wanted to distance themselves from all the troubles at home. Branwell tried again to interest Blackwood's Magazine with his writing, and he sent some of his work to Mr. Wordsworth for his opinion. Nothing came of it, of course. Charlotte sent some of her writing to Mr. Southey, the Poet Laureate, which at least finally received an answer. But that was later.

And I — unable to help in any meaningful way, except to be physically useful in all the housework. I wrote one poem at that time. But I could not share it with Emily. I, too, was grieved by Robert's death, but my poem is but a pale reflection of her despair. I was aware that this was a turning point in our lives, and I tried to show this in a Gondal poem. It was meant to convey this new feeling of my home no longer being a place where I was happy, and my desire to get away. Well, I think we all felt that then, except Emily, who probably wanted to die.*

AB

I will make no comment on that terrible Christmas. It was a nightmare, a vexation of the spirit.

CB

---

* The poem referred to is dated December, 1836, and is entitled Verses by Lady Geralda. To my knowledge it is the earliest one by Anne which she saw fit to save. The last verse reads:
From such a hopeless home to part
Is happiness to me,
For nought can charm my weary heart
Except activity.

I take up my pen again to continue this journal; when I last wrote I was convinced that I would not wish to write more, but life goes on and there have been several events worth recording, one of them rather strange, and another very sad.

The sad event was the violent death of dear Grasper last August. He had been missing for several days. I have no idea how he escaped from the back kitchen, though it may have been my own fault — did I leave the door open? In any case, as soon as I discovered his absence, I asked on all sides if anyone had seen him, but no information was forthcoming until two days later when John Brown told Papa that Grasper had been seen fighting with a strange mongrel down by the Old Hall. Branwell and I, who had been searching and calling for him on the moors above the town, moved our efforts to the bottom of the hill, but again we found nothing. Then on the fourth day, Mr. Brown appeared just before dinner, carrying Grasper's dead body in his arms. He had found him near the river, mangled and lifeless. We assume he must have fought with a large stray and lost. I miss him more than I can say. We buried him in the back yard, as far from the house as possible (at Aunt's insistence), and Papa read a special prayer he had written, praising Grasper's virtues and asking God in His mercy to find a place for him in Heaven. He has promised to find a replacement, but I doubt that any dog can fill the gap in my life left by Grasper.

The strange event I mentioned above occurred in late May. I was in bed, reading over a letter from Anne and thinking about her. The sky was radiant with the glow of the summer evening. I went to the open window and leaned out. A perfect stillness had settled on the world. Not a bird sang or dog barked. The air was filled with the fragrance of new-cut grass. I was still thinking of Anne, whom I had missed terribly all spring. Two years ago we would have been been devising our next adventure and Robert would still have been alive. I was happy then. I was wishing she was at home again, and I called out, very softly, "Anne, Anne, come home…" There was a pause, and then, clear and distinct, I heard her voice, "I am coming… soon." The sound seemed to come from everywhere at once. I sat for a long time after that, pondering these things in my heart. At last I slept, and for once, I slept well.

When Anne came home in June, and we had a moment to ourselves, I asked her if something strange had happened to her in May. She looked at me very oddly and said, "what do you mean, strange?" So I told her what had happened that evening. For a moment she was speechless. "Oh, Em," she said, "I can scarcely believe it. Yes, that is exactly it. I was already in my bed — it must have been after ten o'clock—and just as I was falling asleep I heard your voice very close to me saying 'Anne, come home…' I thought I was dreaming, but I answered at once. The girl in the next bed thought I was talking in my sleep. And I was never sure until now that I was not." We are both pleased and amazed by this occurrence.

Our next diary note was written on Branwell's birthday, the 26th of June. It was very strange to read again the note we had written in 1834; so much has happened since then. We decided to stick to our original plan of recording just that very day, so we wrote that and about our writing, but not about all the terrible events which had happened since the time of our last note. We decided not to mention Roe Head, because then we would have to explain too much — why I left and Anne went in my place. But we felt obliged to include the great national event, the accession to the Throne of the Princess Victoria.

There has been an election, but only Branwell was really interested in it. Papa has become more and more concerned about church matters, which I find rather tedious. We have lost our curate; Mr. Hodgson left us in the spring for a better post. None of us miss him, except Papa, who is forced to work harder and longer than is good for him.

I have been writing a good deal, both stories and poetry. And sometimes I think it is well-written. But really it is mainly for something to keep me from old memories. I still have nightmares about the past, and these I sometimes try to

49

put into poetry though it often becomes confused with the Gondal characters and stories.[*] There was one dream in particular which has stayed with me — it was so vivid: I dreamt I was alone on the moor at twilight — the wind was very strong from the west and the clouds swept across the sky in great streamers, streaked with bloody red, though the sun was already down. I was struggling against the gale to reach the top of the hill but seemed to make no progress. Then, on the path before me I saw Robert. He moved toward me as if he were floating, or being blown by the wind. He looked as he had done in life, tall and muscular, his dark hair curling about his temples, his grey eyes kindling with pleasure. I remember he was even wearing the very jacket, old and threadbare, which he always wore when out on the moors. Suddenly the entire scene changed to night, and now he was resting on a large rock by the path, waiting for me to reach him. But I could not move. I called to him to wait for me but my voice died in my throat. I could see his mouth open as if he were speaking, but I could hear no sound. It was as if there were a great glass wall between us, an impassable barrier. Then I awoke, the tears streaming down my face. This dream has coloured all the succeeding days with overwhelming feelings of horror at my helplessness and loss.

In an effort to overcome this paralysis, I have determined to teach myself the elements of mathematics and geometry, subjects which require intense mental activity,

---

[*] I am struck by one particular theme with which Emily seems obsessed from 1837 – the death of Alexander Elbë. I have found three partial versions of a poem which she began in August, 1837, and which she finally completed at some point, transcribing it into her Gondal Poems book; and she returns to the same theme in a much later poem of December, 1844 ("O Day! He cannot die...") Now that I know that Alexander was one of Robert's alter egos, it is hard not to read these poems as an example of her difficulties in separating Gondal from reality. The last verse of the earlier poem reads:

But thou art now on a desolate sea –
Parted from Gondal and parted from me –
All my repining is hopeless and vain,
Death never yields back his victims again – Ed.

and which, to some extent, keep at bay unwanted thoughts and feelings. And it is a very absorbing study indeed. Papa has borrowed some elementary books from the Mechanics Institute for me as well as lending me his own Euclid. He has also begun to teach me Latin, and we are now beginning the Aeneid. Branwell continually mocks my feeble attempts at translation, but he is not malicious and often helps me with difficult passages.

Aunt, on the other hand, has withdrawn almost completely. I think we barely exchange two words in a day. But worst of all, she and Tabby are forever arguing. I don't know how long I can stand this.

EJB

I for one thought that Emily was recovering well from her ordeal of the previous December. Over the summer we had written a great deal of Gondal material, and she seemed cheerful and serene. Only occasionally at night did I see any evidence that she was not at peace. She would never tell me her nightmares, and I felt it must have been still too painful for her to speak of. And she really did make enormous progress both in her music and her study of mathematics and Latin. Yet her rather forced cheerfulness did give me some unease; it seemed incredible that she had recovered so quickly.

AB

During the summer of 1837 I fear I must admit that Emily's state of mind was far from foremost in my thoughts. I dreaded my return to Roe Head — it loomed before me, a gigantic dark prison, and I felt myself shrinking before the image, wholly inadequate to perform my duties there, fearful of my own weaknesses, and unworthy to be trusted with the responsibilities of teaching these young know-nothings. I longed to be free, and to spend time with my dear friend Ellen. I needed rest and reassurance that summer, but the situation at home was far from pleasant. Papa was over-worked and preoccupied with politics; Branwell had his own companions and was moving away from me and all our old pursuits; Anne and Emily were always together, excluding me from their 'games', and of course, Aunt Branwell continued to be critical and short-tempered. I had hoped that at least Ellen might be able to visit, but even that was denied me as she was very involved in her own family problems at the time. If it had not been for my writing, I think I would have had serious thoughts of terminating my wretched existence.

 One last comment: although I knew nothing at the time of the strange psychic link between Emily and Anne in the summer of 1837, Emily and Anne did relate this episode to me at a much later date, when we were all at work on our novels. It provided me with a much-needed device to bring Jane Eyre back to Thornfield, and though this was severely criticised as being over-romantic and quite unbelievable, I know that such things happen…

CB

_____

Today it has been exactly one year since Robert was buried. I marked the day by putting a few poor sprigs of heather on his grave. But I feel strangely numb, as if I were wrapped in a blanket of misery which shuts out the world — everything seems far away. It is a kind of paralysis and I have no will to act. Somehow the chores get done, but I often forget doing them, and sometimes even start to sweep the rooms again, having only just finished. I have given up my studies for the moment, all except the piano. For a while after Robert's death I had abundant energy, though I became very thin. Everyone thought I was recovering easily. Now I only want to sleep.

I wrote a long poem yesterday and today, however.[*] It carried on with a plot Robert and I had begun to work out years ago. But it has turned into a very sad affair — my heroine is dying. How I envy her.

Anne and Charlotte are home early from Roe Head. They both appear to be ill, but I have not the energy to inquire about the details.

I miss Grasper.

EJB

---

[*] The sad poem referred to here is dated 14 December 1837, and begins:

O mother, I am not regretting
To leave this wretched world below,
If there be nothing but forgetting
In that dark land to which I go   Ed.

Anne has just returned to Roe Head. She has been at home for several months. I fear I didn't realize at first that this was the result of a serious illness and deep melancholy. Charlotte has also been at home, also suffering from depressed spirits, but otherwise well enough. The two of them left us last week, both looking very disconsolate. I believe Anne's condition was entirely due to exhaustion from over-work combined with her ridiculous conviction that she was going to die and not go to heaven. I wish she would stop listening to those harsh clerics of Mirfield whose only pleasure in life seems to be to terrify their congregations with the wages of sin and the fear of damnation. But she is a brave girl; when she was most ill and in fear of her life, she asked to see the Moravian minister who then wisely and kindly reminded her of the love of Christ, and reassured her that 'the gift of eternal life' would surely be hers. I kept my own thoughts on this matter to myself as they would have only distressed Anne. But at least in this Journal I can confess that I begin to find the entire Christian story singularly unconvincing.

Christmas was brightened, however, by a new addition to the family — Papa had finally found a suitable replacement for Grasper. When we were all gathered around the breakfast table on Christmas morning, Papa disappeared into the back of the house, and returned with the most charming and lively puppy. He is part mastiff, and will be quite terrifying when he grows up. We were all thrilled, except for Aunt, who grumbled about letting a dog into the dining room. But Papa over-ruled her; he knew we all needed cheering up, and he was excited as a little boy over our new guardian. He joked and read a passage from Sir Walter's *The Talisman* to her, "Recollect that the Almighty, who gave the dog to be companion of our pleasures and our toils, hath invested him with a nature noble and incapable of deceit." Very appropriate, and Aunt was duly put in her place. We are going to call him Keeper, as he will be the

manic-depressive

keeper of our safety and all our worldly goods, like a true friend and protector. I am to be allowed to train him, with Papa's help.

EJB

The tone of this entry, so unlike the previous one, bothers me greatly. Although Emily appears to have recovered her animal spirits, she sounds false, as if she were, perhaps unconsciously, pretending to be happier that she actually was. It has caused me to remember that when I was sent home from Roe Head in November (Charlotte accompanied me) because of illness, I found Emily distinctly distant. Her letters had been full of small homely events, and she was apparently coping very well with her grief. It pained me to think that after our psychic communication in May, and the long summer holiday of intense Gondal activity, she had become hard and unfeeling toward me. But perhaps it was only that my own feelings were hurt; I wanted to tell her about my illness and unhappiness, and my worries about salvation and damnation, but she wouldn't listen, and perhaps I should have realized that she was still recovering (in her peculiar way) from the events of the previous year. She seemed to want to pretend that everything was as it should be, and that I should make more of an effort to rise above this 'weakness'. I realize that she had lost all faith in God at the time of Robert's death, so I must forgive her, but I am deeply saddened that this mainstay of life was not available to her when she needed it most. Nevertheless, her remarks in this Journal about my own religious faith were hurtful indeed.

AB

Having just read over Emily's version of the year 1837 and then Anne's comments, I realize that I was completely unaware of their inner worlds. My own year had been so fraught with anguished melancholy, I simply did not notice Anne's distress until she fell ill. Then I went too far and briefly made an enemy of Miss Wooler, accusing her of insensitivity and callousness. I can hardly say what ailed me, I felt so unworthy, quite beyond salvation. And I found myself falling ever downwards into my stories to escape the harsh reality around me. Finally being at home after the torture of Roe Head I was happy to forget the outside world which had become so alien and unfriendly. And I was quite satisfied that Emily's apparent equanimity was genuine. At the end of the summer, I was persuaded to return to Roe Head; Miss Wooler really did need and love me, and I have a compulsion to supply help when it is asked for. But I am not able to supply help when it is needed but <u>not</u> asked for, as was the case both with Anne and Emily that year. I could not help it.

CB

I write because I am absolutely furious! Aunt has started again to insist that I should be looking for a husband or a position. She seems to have not the slightest awareness that without me at home, none of the kitchen or cleaning work would ever be done. Tabby is still so infirm that she can accomplish only a small fraction of what she was able to do before her accident. Aunt spends so much time in her room now that she seems to have no idea what is happening in the house. In fact, I think she would only have her just deserts if I left her to do the heavy work herself. Of course, that is not what would happen. She would simply let Tabby shoulder the whole burden, and that might kill her, or she would hire another servant, which Papa cannot afford. Anne says that it would be dreadful for none of us to stay at home, but she thinks that at least two of us must soon be earning some money. And I suppose one might as well be me. And in any case, it would be eminently sensible for Anne (who returned home in March, just before Miss Wooler transferred her school to Dewsbury Moor) to be at home for a while; not only has she been away for over two years, but she also will be good for Aunt, who loves her best. I know Charlotte would also like to stay at home, but she and Aunt have never been on the best of terms, and I think she is the most employable of us all, even though she hates teaching — perhaps she would have more success as a private governess. She has finished with Dewsbury Moor, and says she will not return.

We have just had a visit from Charlotte's two school friends, Mary and Martha Taylor. This was surprisingly stimulating — they are both intelligent and interesting girls, very outspoken. Mary in particular has extreme radical views, many of which I find both daring and yet oddly congenial. She strongly supports the thesis that unmarried women should always be self-supporting — that it is their duty. She upbraided me for being such a stay-at-home while Charlotte has been working herself into an early grave. I defended myself as best I could, but I fear that I am guilty of the charge. At least Mary has further energized me into taking some action to find employment.

Martha is completely charming, full of the joy of life, bubbling with excitement at every new sight or sound. Both girls are accomplished pianists, especially Mary. We played and sang together as often as Papa would allow us the use of his study. I think Branwell is quite taken with Mary, and watches her with calf-eyes when she is at the piano. Very amusing. They left us two days ago, and we feel very flat now.

Speaking of Branwell, there is a plan afoot to set him up in Bradford as a professional portraitist. As he is only moderately talented, I don't see how he will ever support even himself, but he shows no signs of being able to bring in any cash except by painting. Yet again Branwell is favoured, though it is hardly surprising. I only wish he were more thorough and business-like in his work. I can well imagine him in Bradford, making as many friends as possible and neglecting his chosen field of endeavour, to the detriment of us all.

As for Aunt's desire to see me married, she may as well wish for the moon. She still seems to believe that James Greenwood might wish to marry me, in spite of all, and cannot understand that even if that were the case — which it is not, as far as I know — I am now perfectly sure that I do not ever, EVER wish to marry. If I cannot marry for love, then what is the point? The temptation to marry for comfort and rank was put before me, and I was punished accordingly for ever considering it. And I will never love another as I loved Robert. His loss is ever in my mind. I sometimes dream that we are together, and I think in that dream state, "Oh, you have returned — now we will be happy at last!" And then, even in my dream, I realize that he is dead, and I have crossed over into his world, and that I am dead, too. I awake from these dreams with the odd feeling that he really visited me in my sleep (or I visited him perhaps), and that this is a portent of what is to come. But the harsh reality of the dawning day soon intrudes, and I know I must wash and dress, and face the familiar routine of my daily chores.

So my path in this world appears, therefore, quite clear. I can only satisfy everyone's needs by leaving home and finding paid employment. To be free from Aunt's constant reproaches would be worth a very great sacrifice on my part, and it would please Papa if I could help with the family finances. Anne can stay at home and help Tabby, and Charlotte can take her time in finding a better position. But what kind of employment am I fit for? I suppose I could learn to teach, if some kind soul would be willing to risk giving me the opportunity.

EJB

What a pity things didn't work out as she hoped. But the summer at least was pleasant, I recall. Peaceful. And I rejoiced in being free again.

AB

I was so pleased to read this entry — I had no idea how much Emily appreciated Mary and Martha Taylor, and what an effect Mary had on her decision to seek employment. Emily made very few decisions in her life; indeed she usually just went along with the plans of others, so long as they didn't inconvenience her own personal inclinations. Looking for a position seemed quite a dramatic and uncharacteristic step for her. But of course, at that time, she didn't know I would be returning to Miss Wooler, and I did not know that she felt it was her turn to leave home.

CB

Much to my amazement, my response to an advertisement in the Leeds Intelligencer for a young female teacher has yielded a positive reply! A very respectable establishment in Southowram is in urgent need of a novice teacher. The letter from Miss Elizabeth Patchett of Law Hill arrived this morning, requesting me to present myself there for an interview at my earliest convenience. Papa will accompany me in the village phaeton — he and Aunt both say it would be inappropriate to appear unaccompanied and on foot. We set off tomorrow morning.

August, 1838

The interview was surprisingly agreeable. Miss Patchett is a very distinguished lady, highly accomplished and intelligent. She quizzed me on my education, and was not at all surprised to learn that I had been educated at home primarily by my father, and was rather impressed by my progress in mathematics and music. Papa somewhat exaggerated my abilities in those departments, I think — I hope she will not be disappointed. By the end of the interview she pronounced that I appeared to fit her requirements, and I was accepted on the spot. I take up my new post in two weeks. Papa and Aunt are very pleased. Anne is also pleased, though we will miss each other, and Charlotte is both pleased and surprised. I think she thought I had fallen so deep in the Slough that I would never extricate myself.

EJB

I remember thinking, that summer, that perhaps everything was going to turn out for the best after all — I was finished with school and was so glad to be at home again — and Emily was at last beginning to think about the future. Papa was pleased that it appeared most of us were at least beginning to be able to earn some money — Branwell set up in Bradford as a professional painter, Charlotte still wanted at Dewsbury Moor, and Emily about to start a career as a teacher in Southowram. I was considered too young to work. How odd. In the end I was the only one to succeed as a governess. I take some satisfaction in that. It seems a small thing now, especially after Charlotte's great success with her novel, but though I may not have the genius of the others, I am proud that I kept my post longer than any of my siblings.

AB

July, 1849

Poor Anne — she worked so hard and had so little reward for all her labour. I pray that her faith in the Life Everlasting will be justified. She of all of us deserves a place in Heaven.

C Brontë

64

It is so good to be at home again. Keeper was overjoyed to see me. He has been very naughty while I was away, and no one is able to control him. So my first task is to teach him never to sleep on the beds, and then he must learn to obey orders from Tabby as well as Papa.

Papa is not very well, very over-worked and worried. I wish he would find a new curate.

But the saddest news greeted me on my return: Anne Greenwood has died. I long to visit Spring Head, to comfort the bereaved, and help with the household arrangements. But I know I would not be welcome. Papa has been there several times, and does his best to comfort Mr. Joseph. He says that William and James are both distressed, particularly William who adored his little sister. James was closer to Sarah, but with her gone, he, like William, doted on Anne. My God, first Sarah and now Anne. How can they bear it? And poor Martha is quite distracted, and hardly seems to be aware of her surroundings. She has always been unstable, but now, according to Papa, she cries and then laughs insanely and appears to be completely witless. They have had to shut her up in her bedroom most of the time so that she doesn't wander out and stray into the river. She has already had one watery excursion from which she was saved in the nick of time by one of the mill operatives who happened to be passing. And only last week she set fire to her curtains while trying to light a candle on the window ledge. She seemed to think that Anne was out in the dark, all alone, and she wanted to help her find her way home. Oh, if there were only some way I could help. But even if I could, it would only be for a short time — I am expected back at Law Hill before the end of January.

And now I must admit that I am not looking forward to returning. My first term as a teacher has not been an unqualified success. I have tried very hard to do all that is required, but I find it both exhausting and tedious. The children are not bad, but they are not very intelligent nor are they obedient. And my duties include several very uncongenial services such as mending, which I hate and for which I have no aptitude, and reading aloud to the younger children. The latter task would be quite enjoyable except that the little imps plague me with comments and questions, and never want to hear the stories I wish to read. They are always demanding that I read such nonsense as Bulwer's The Last Days of Pompeii. Has Scott already gone completely out of fashion? However, I have managed to find time for my own writing, and have even written one or two verses which please me.[*] I have also kept up the Gondal Sagas, though it is difficult without Anne's help. But the urge to escape to Gondal when surrounded by unruly and stupid pupils is all but irresistible.

escape!

---

[*] Emily wrote a great number of poems during her first term at Law Hill, at least two of which were inspired by her Gondal Sagas. But, more interestingly, she was beginning to write very personal verse; indeed the very first poem to be transcribed into her book of private poems (written in November 1938) describes her longing for home and for the happy 'time when no labour nor dreaming/Broke the sleep of the happy and free.' But the most moving verse of all is clearly about Robert:

O Dream, where are thou now?
Long years have past away
Since last, from off thine angel brow
I saw the light decay.

What else cd this be about?

Alas, alas for me
Thou wert so bright and fair,
I could not think thy memory
Would yield me nought but care!

The sun-beam and the storm,
The summer-eve devine,
The silent night of solemn calm,
The full moon's cloudless shine,

Were once entwined with thee,
But now with weary pain,
Lost vision! 'tis enough for me –
Thou canst not shine again.   Ed.

Charlotte is home for good; she has decided finally not to return to Dewsbury Moor. There may have been some unpleasantness.

EJB

She was certainly correct — my last days at Dewsbury Moor were agony! Indeed, Dewsbury Moor will ever be enshrined in my memory as a place of tedium, drudgery, and unhappiness. I did my best to satisfy Miss Wooler, but the labour of teaching, looking after young children and old folk, and generally running the school was too much for my constitution. I had tried twice before to leave this employment, and finally Miss W agreed that it was necessary for my health to finally call a halt to my labours. She turned the school over to her sister, so at least I did not feel that I was betraying her personal trust.

CB

Home again, under a cloud. I am entirely to blame — not because I was wrong, but because I lost my temper. Oh dear, what is to become of me? And it was over such a small thing. Miss Patchett asked me to teach several of her little darlings the elements of the pianoforte. Well, I would agree, I said, but that I would have to be relieved of some of my other duties to find the time. And then she said that would be impossible as Miss Hartley and Miss Aspden were already fully occupied with their own work. I knew this to be true so I acquiesced — access to a piano, I thought, was too tempting to ignore. After two weeks it became obvious that I was failing in my other duties. Miss Patchett then reproached me for being too slow in all the mending I was required to do, and at that moment I lost my temper. I turned on her in fury, saying I had warned her that I would not be able to teach piano and accomplish everything else she expected of me, and that if she wanted me to continue, she would either have to hire a seamstress or insist that her pupils be required to do their own mending. I knew as I said it that I had gone too far. Very quietly she said, "In that case, Miss Brontë, I think it is time you looked for other employment."

So now I am home again, and again I am in disgrace. And to make matters worse, Anne has decided to go out as a governess. She has already found a place with a very respectable family, and leaves next month.

Both Branwell and Charlotte are also at home now; Branwell, as I expected, was unable to make a go of his career as a painter of portraits. Well, at least I have company in my disgrace!

EJB

Now at last I understand what happened at Law Hill. Emily was always very vague about why she left; I never dreamed she had actually been dismissed. All she ever said was that it was urgent for her health that she return home. This explains much of what happened later in connection with our school plan. Of course I knew that she wasn't fond of teaching, but I see now why she never tried to obtain another post — and in any case, Miss Patchett would never have given her a reference after such an outburst.

AB

Emily did tell me, much later, what had happened at Law Hill. We were in Brussels and Mme Heger asked her to teach some of the younger children the piano. Emily reacted very badly to the request (although, with my help, she eventually agreed, on her terms), and then explained to me why she was so reluctant — it was because of her experience at Law Hill — and she feared she would lose patience again, just when she was making such progress on all fronts in her own education. I have often thought that Emily's temper, which could be terrifying, was a trait she inherited from Papa. I remember as a child cowering with the others in our little study, listening to his violent outbursts at Nancy or Sarah Garrs over the most trivial matters. He always regretted it, and like Emily, was the first to recognize this failing. But I think we all learned very early to be quiet and obedient children, mainly for fear of arousing his wrath.

CB

The year is drawing to its close, and I think it is time to sum up events since last I wrote. For myself, I have been content to be at home. I begin to feel that I may never leave. Aunt at last seems resigned that I will never marry, and Papa is glad to have me about the place. Papa is much relieved to have found a new curate — Mr. Weightman— who came at the end of the summer. He is a veritable paragon of beauty and wit. Charlotte is quite taken with him, which she hides under a thick veneer of satire and sally. As for myself, I feel nothing but friendship toward him, and we have had many a spirited exchange on philosophical topics. Although we agree on many subjects, we had a serious parting of the ways last week — I maintaining that there were profound contradictions between the Old and New Testaments, which weakened the authority of both, and he claiming that the New Testament only expanded and improved on the Old, taking God's message to a larger congregation, refining and amplifying the simple laws of Moses with the subtle teachings of Christ. My own feeling is that the Old Testament is bigoted and puritanical, and the New is so impossible to live up to, that a 'true' Christian will always be overwhelmed with guilt and inferiority. Or he will be a 'good' Christian, in other words, a hypocrite — something I see about me at every turn.

Other events of interest — Charlotte has been a temporary governess for the Sidgwicks in Lothersdale. I think she was prejudiced against them from the beginning as Mrs. S is good friends with Papa's old antagonist, Mr. James Greenwood of Woodlands. She is also his distant cousin. I wonder how much Mrs. S knows about my aborted connection with young James of Spring Head? In any event, Charlotte had some very interesting experiences, including a few weeks at the summer home of Mrs. Sidgwick's very wealthy father, John Greenwood — he has a grand house called Swarcliffe not far from Harrogate. She told us all about it, the beautiful clothes, the exotic and elegant dinners, the elaborate games. But as she, the governess, was excluded

71

from taking part in any of this gaiety, she is glad to be at home again. She also had a wonderful holiday — her first— at Burlington with Ellen Nussey. Charlotte looks very well now, and seems genuinely happy for the first time in several years. But, although I'm sure the holiday did her good, I think another reason for her high spirits is that she has had two proposals of marriage! The first was last March when she had a letter from Henry Nussey, Ellen's brother, suggesting that she should marry him as she would be a good Christian helpmate to him. We all laughed, Charlotte most of all. He clearly does not know her very well; I'm sure he would be shocked and scandalized if he knew about her secret passion for story-writing. She sent him a very tactful letter refusing him, however, as she doesn't want to offend Ellen. The second proposal was much more romantic, and came from Mr. Hodgson's friend, Mr. Pryce. He is a lively Irishman, who has met her only once (on a visit with Mr. Hodgson, our old curate) but was smitten on the spot. He proposed by letter a few weeks after his visit. Extraordinary! In a way this was the reverse of Henry N.'s proposal, although both are clergymen in need of a wife. Henry thought only of the practicalities of the match, while Mr. Pryce's letter was full admiration for her wit and imagination. I think Charlotte briefly considered the latter proposal as possible, but decided against it as it was clear that the man has a weak constitution, which, coupled with our own family tendencies, bodes ill for a successful marriage. Also she didn't find him particularly attractive. But there is no denying that she is quite buoyed up by the unexpected admiration. Aunt, bless her, is astounded at this turn of events; she always said that Charlotte was the least likely of all of us to find a husband!

Anne has just come home from Blake Hall— they have told her she is not to return. It is her first failure. None of us can understand in what way she has disappointed them. She is very dispirited, but I am not sorry she is back with me; Gondal is in a sad state, though I have been writing like fury all year. Now together we will bring the scoundrels up to the scratch. Also, we need her at home. Tabby has finally admitted she is not capable of her work, and her leg is so badly ulcerated that she cannot stand for more than a few minutes. She and her sister have acquired a small house in the village where they now live. I visit every day. Little Martha Brown comes in to help us, but it requires the efforts of all of us to keep up with the cleaning, sewing, ironing, and cooking. Aunt is a hard task-master, and I know Tabby is thankful that she can now take things easy.

Branwell has at last taken a step toward independence. He leaves us on the last day of the year to take up a post as tutor to the sons of a Mr. Postlethwaite in Broughton-in-Furness. I hope that he will succeed, but I am not sanguine.

There has been a major change of a surprising kind in the parish of Bradford — the new vicar is none other than the famous Dr. William Scoresby! Papa is delighted, and has been to meet him. Dr. Scoresby, according to Papa, is most impressive — very decisive and masterful. He has great plans for the Parish, not all of which will he find easy to execute — but he and Papa seem to agree on most of them. I fear, however, that the Church Rate controversy, which has unsettled the Parish for many years, will be his undoing. I despair of an amicable solution to this conundrum. The underlying problem is the ambiguous nature of the Established Church. Because it has secular as well as religious functions, Papa and Dr. Scoresby want the Church Rate paid by all, but because most of the funds are used in the upkeep and repair of the Churches, the Dissenters (especially the Baptists) are vigorously opposed. On top of this, there is the dispute between the Church in Bradford and the various chapelries in Bradford Parish, who object to Bradford taking the lion's share of all the moneys. Haworth is particularly disadvantaged in this way. And the various precedents and statutes in church and civil law only complicate the matter further. It is chaos. Dr. Scoresby will have to be very wary in how he deals with this, and very clever. Papa has invited him to dine with us early in the new year and perhaps we will learn how he plans to handle this hornet's nest.

On the third anniversary of Robert's funeral, a few days

73

ago, I went as usual to stand at his graveside. He lies next to his brother. I hope they are united in death as they were in life. I wrote a short poem today to commemorate their sad, short lives.[*]

I have just read over this last entry, and see clearly that I am becoming a very sedate person, with no visible life of my own. I had intended this Journal to be my confidant, the holder of precious thoughts and secrets, and now I find it has become nothing more than a gazette of passing events. Well, I cannot help it. If I recorded all my dreams and nightmares it would become grotesque, and if I recorded the events in the Gondal Histories, I would only be repeating the vast quantities of fiction in which Anne and I have been engrossed in writing for two years. My verse is also recorded elsewhere, so I may as well terminate this journal, as it seems to be surplus to requirements.

Emily Jane Brontë

---

[*] The poem to which Emily refers was written on the 19 December, 1839, it is strange, even uncanny, to realize that she wrote these two brief verses on death exactly 9 years before her own demise. It reads:

Heavens glory shone where he was laid
In lifes decline
I turned me from that young saints bed
To gaze on thine –

It was a summer day that saw
His spirits flight
Thine parted in a time of awe
A winter-night.

74

Emily mentions my dismissal by the Inghams of Blake Hall as being unexplained. Actually I knew perfectly well why I was not asked to return — I simply was unable to discipline the little monsters, and so was unable to teach them. Charlotte understood my plight to some extent, blaming the children and their parents for not supporting me in my efforts, but I am compelled in all honesty to admit I was too inexperienced and too sensitive to handle such robust and lively creatures. I thought that all children were like us when we were little; obedient, quiet, studious — except for Emily, and even she was pretty well-behaved at home, most of the time. But I learned a great deal at Blake Hall which stood me in good stead at Thorp Green. I surmounted my short-comings there, I think.

As for Mr. Weightman, well, I think we all succumbed to his charm, not just Charlotte and I. Emily said she was impervious to his gallantry and saw him only as a friend, but I certainly detected a slight gleam in her eye whenever he was about. I know I thought at the time that he fancied her, but her manner with him was more like a comrade than a sweetheart, and in the end they were more like brother and sister. Yet in reading over Emily's poems, I noticed one written in October, 1839, which certainly suggests to me that she seemed more hopeful about her chances of finding a new love, in spite of all that had happened three years before. The last two verses were:

Yet could I with past pleasures,
Past woe's oblivion buy—
That by the death of my dearest treasures
My deadliest pains might die,

O then another daybreak
Might haply dawn above—
Another summer gild my cheek,
My Soul, another love—

Of course, she was never able to completely put those terrible events of the winter of 1836 behind her, but certainly it seems that she was beginning in 1839 to think it might be possible.

AB

I am very surprised to read the above comments by Anne; I never realized that Emily might herself have been interested in W.W. But I have to admit that Emily's comments on my own interest in him hit the mark squarely, as did her account of my 'suitors'. That golden period from August, 1839, to March, 1841, was probably one of the happiest of my life.

But if Emily were also regaining her customary cheerful outlook by the end of the year 1839, as Anne seems to think, it was surely a fragile and delicate plant, and could not survive for long under the endless onslaught of her sad memories. I, too, have been studying Emily's poetry for that year and am particularly struck by one which she wrote in May. It is imbued with loneliness, regret, disillusionment, and even guilt. And it clearly refers to that terrible time of Robert Clayton's death, as it speaks of her 19th year. The last two verses are:

First melted off the hope of youth
Then Fancy's rainbow fast withdrew
And then experience told me truth
In mortal bosoms never grew.

'Twas grief enough to think mankind
All hollow, servile, insincere[*]
But worse to trust to my own mind
And find the same corruption there.

Is it fanciful to think that perhaps she felt a gnawing guilt for her behaviour toward her two suitors? It certainly appears to

---

[*] Emily first wrote this line using the words, 'hollow, servile' but crossed them out. I have reinstated them simply because she never re-visited this poem.

76

me that by the time she had apparently decided between them, it was too late and Robert was dead — how could she not have felt that she betrayed them both? I am quite sure that Edgar Linton and the young Heathcliff must have sprung to life from the ashes of her remorse over Robert's death and her frivolous flirtation with poor James Greenwood.

CB

No, I must try again. Am I so hardened and ageing that all springs of hopeful youth have dried up? I have lately read over my verses of the past year — they were written quickly and some are more true than I had realized. Memories of the past inform them all. The present seems to have little significance for me and my feelings are alive only in dreams and in memory. Everything around me seems pale and empty, drained of any joy or sadness. Only in dreams do I regain living pain or pleasure. Sometimes when I wake in the early hours of the morning, I long to revisit the past so intensely I think I sense its presence. Lately I thought I could see Robert's face just outside my window, but when I lept from my bed to open it, he had vanished. I suppose I might have been dreaming. Or that I want to see him again so much that I imagine I see his face everywhere. I know it is useless to always be looking for him – he is gone now and will not come back. Yet I find it impossible to accept that I will never see him again, and a small voice in my head keeps saying 'someday you will be together, after you too are dead'. Dare I hope that this is true?

I have talked to Anne about this, but all she can offer is the Christian hope of life everlasting. We seem to be drifting apart. The whole idea of living this life for some heavenly reward seems ridiculous to me. All I want is to go back to those happy years when I was young and alive and in love. That would be my heaven.

I think Anne has hopes that Mr. Weightman will notice her, but he seems oblivious of her existence. We are all lumped together in his mind, I think, as those three ugly sisters.

I wish spring would come. Then at least I could get away from this house and take Keeper for a run on the moors. Today has been cold and grey and threatens more snow. The sky is leaden, and the streets slippery with old snow, soot, and slime from the middens. This is a disgusting town.

But there is one cheerful event to record: last week Dr. and Mrs. Scoresby came to dinner, as promised. I was astounded to learn that he knew all the great men of science, and is himself one of the world's experts on the phenomenon of Magnetism. But I was particularly interested in his tales of whaling and his explorations and researches in the Arctic. I wish I had had the courage to ask him all the questions that were buzzing about in my head.*

After dinner Papa and Dr. Scoresby were closeted in Papa's study for over an hour while we entertained Mrs. Scoresby in the dining room. She is an Irish lady of good Anglican family (Papa was quite taken with her), but very delicate. I thought her rather too inclined to complain — she is quite appalled by the rude manners of her husband's parishioners. I wonder what she would think if she could hear Mr. Winterbotham on the subject of the Vicar of Bradford?!**

EJB

---

* William Scoresby, Jr., the eminent whaling captain and scientist, was the Vicar of Bradford Parish from 1839 to 1846. He is best known as the author of *An Account of the Arctic Regions* (1820).   Ed.

** William Winterbotham was the Baptist minister of Haworth's West Lane Chapel from 1831 to 1841. He was Scoresby's and my father's most vociferous opponent in the famous Haworth and Bradford Church Rate disputes. Ed.

Apparently Emily's hopeful mood evaporated in that winter of 1839-40. Recently I turned again to her poetry to try to find some clue as to what had happened, but only found deeply sad verses, all harking back to Robert's death. She seemed to turn in on herself more and more. Although we were still working on the Gondal Chronicles, she had ceased to confide in me anything of a personal nature. Perhaps she felt I was betraying her in looking for another position, but even she agreed that this was necessary. I fear the real reason was that while I retained a strong Christian faith, she felt there was no one she could talk to about her own doubts and distress. She had always before given some credence to the hope of life after death, but at that time she seemed to doubt even that. This was a very difficult time for me; I myself needed comfort and Emily was in no mood to give it. Sometime in January I learned through Charlotte of the death of my little friend, Anne Cook.* We had been very close at Roe Head, and we corresponded for a while after I left. But I did not speak of it to Emily — it would have been pointless.

AB

I feel such guilt over that period now. Sometimes I wonder if Emily sank into her black moods because I was so happy at that time. But I was oblivious, of both her and Anne. What little I remember of that winter is that I was much engrossed by Ellen and Mary's affairs, not to mention Wm. W. And I think I recall that Aunt was very short-tempered much of the time, mainly because Tabby had left us, so housework had become more of a chore for everyone. And we had various visitors as well, which Emily always hated (with the obvious exception of Dr. Scoresby). Or perhaps she was just irritated by all of us being at home. Anne and I were both looking for positions, but I admit I was not trying as hard as I might have. Well, it's water under the bridge now, and regrets are futile.

CB

---

* Anne Cook (1825-1840) was both a friend of Anne and a pupil of mine at Roe Head. She was a handsome girl, warm-hearted and affectionate. Ed.

I must here record some recent events which, in our quiet and uneventful lives, are so out of the ordinary they need careful recording for posterity. And who should they concern but our faithful Celia-Amelia (Charlotte's pet name for the divine William Weightman). He has quite gone out of his way to organize us into a spirit of fun and rebellion! While dear Ellen Nussey was visiting us recently, he discovered that none of us had ever received a Valentine (what a surprise...) and he proceeded to write us each a poem of unqualified admiration (mine was 'O Soul Divine'!) then he walked all the way to Bradford to post them so we (and Aunt) shouldn't know who had sent them — as if it could have been anyone else. And to further entertain us, he arranged for an invitation to be sent from Keighley, inviting us all (including Ellen) to tea with Mr. Collins and his wife, and to attend C-A's lecture at the Mechanics Institute in the evening. His subject was 'The Advantages of Classical Studies', a topic close to both his and Papa's hearts. It was clever and amusing, but it always strikes me as very odd that Christian Clergymen put so much store by pre-Christian philosophy and literature. In any case, it was a splendid excursion. We didn't manage to arrive home until near midnight, accompanied by W.W. and Mr. Collins, who had both been very gallant and lively on the long climb back to Haworth. Aunt, of course, was furious. The very idea of four unmarried girls being accompanied by a dashing bachelor and a married man unaccompanied by his wife convinced her that we were all fast on the road to perdition. She had prepared hot coffee for us four girls, and nearly refused to serve any to the gentlemen, even though we were all blue with cold from our long walk. But W.W. teased and flattered her into submission, and the gentlemen were finally rewarded with steaming cups. Although Aunt has been cross and irritable ever since, Papa was highly amused.

EJB

I can see Emily now, a quiet smile lurking behind her grey eyes, ready with a terse but witty response to the nonsense being spouted by Mr. W. and Mr. C. We were so gay that evening — a time to remember and treasure forever.

AB

I had nearly forgotten about all that, so much has happened since. Yet it all comes back now with renewed poignancy. Now Emily and William Weightman are both in their graves, and Anne is failing daily.

By the by, Mr. Collins turned out a very bad penny — only a few years ago we learned that he had deserted his poor wife, leaving her destitute in Manchester with the children, and escaping his debts by going off to the Continent for a life of debauchery. Horrible man.

CB

The past year has been eventful for at least two in the family. The news concerning Branwell, however, is not very encouraging. He was dismissed by Mr. Postlethwaite in June, and has been very secretive as to the cause. Anne and I are sure, from his veiled hints, that he must have taken advantage of a female house servant, and Mr. P found out, dismissing them both. Papa has had a letter from Mr. P but it is very vague as to the reason for the dismissal. Perhaps he felt in some way that he could have prevented it, or at least that Branwell was only partly to blame. The irony of the situation is rather striking — Papa and Aunt saved me from a similar fate ('ruin'), by separating me from Robert, so ruining my life, while Branwell was not saved and only lost his position. Of course, men are never 'ruined', only a little embarrassed. And to top it all, he has already found a new post, this time with the Leeds and Manchester Railway as 'assistant clerk-in-charge'. Hardly a fitting post for a classically educated artist and poet, but needs must... I only hope he will take his duties seriously this time.

As for myself, it has been a fruitful if not a happy year. I have begun to write tolerable verse, and much of it is in no way connected with Gondal. I think this is a forward step, even though the best of my poems still hark back to my childhood and youth, and to the great tragedy which overtook me in my 19th year. I copy out one of them; it painfully illustrates my point:

> It is too late to call thee now—
> I will not nurse that dream again
> For every joy that lit my brow
> Would bring its after storm of pain—
>
> Besides the mist is half withdrawn,
> The barren mountain-side lies bare
> And sunshine and awaking morn
> Paint no more golden visions there—

Yet ever in my grateful breast
Thy darling shade shall cherished be
For God alone doth know how blest
My early years have been in thee!*

In May, Anne left home again, this time to be a governess near York. She was very efficient in finding new employment, and very suitable it is. She now lives in a beautiful home in beautiful countryside, has the care and education of three little girls; and the family she serves is both wealthy and well-educated. The father, Edmund Robinson, is a clergyman (though not 'practising') and landed gentry. The mother is the daughter of the famous Thomas Gisborne. Papa is delighted as he is a great admirer of Gisborne, a classic Evangelical, and friend of his old mentor, William Wilberforce. I know this is for the best, but I cannot help feeling bereft yet again.

Charlotte has been at home since the summer of last year. She has been much occupied by the search for a suitable position, but has yet to find one to her liking. She is enjoying being at home, and seems to be in no hurry to leave it. I wonder whether the presence of one Celia-Amelia may be having some influence on her... He has certainly won the hearts of every eligible maiden in both Keighley and Haworth parish. Even Anne blushes and stammers whenever he addresses her. I hope she is not allowing her hopes to rise — his affections at the moment appear to centre on a Miss Walton of Appleby of whom he speaks rapturously, and I

---

* This poem was written in April, 1840. Another poem of this period is the very moving short piece, 'If grief for grief can touch thee...', written in May, 1840. This last verse expresses the hope of reunion:

Yea, by the tears I've poured
By all my hours of pain,
O, I shall surely win thee,
Beloved, again!   Ed.

think they have an understanding. Poor Anne. She would dearly love to be married and produce half a dozen children.

EJB

Dearest Emily, if only you knew how much I am touched by your concern. I didn't dream that you were so aware of my great longing for a family, and my interest in W.W. I knew that it would come to nothing, — he was far too 'eligible' to be interested in me or Charlotte. You, on the other hand, might have captured his heart if only you had tried.

And I never knew that you missed me when I went away to Thorp Green — you had been so remote when I was at home. If only you had said something. Your letters to me while I was away were always full of amusing incident but said very little about your personal feelings. I have saved them all, and reading that particular group over, I am still unable to detect any indication of your real feelings.

AB

The following letter from Emily was enclosed here by Anne:

Haworth
20 August 1840

Dearest Anne,

Since you were last at home nothing of serious interest has occurred, but you may be amused by a tale of Mr. W.W. and his bevy of admirers. You would never believe it, but apparently Sarah Sugden (Sarah the Sausage) has set her cap for him. Was he tempted by her money and rank? All I know for sure is that she invited him to a grand ball at Eastwood House, and was refused.* Poor girl. All the money in the world would not tempt our Celia-Amelia unless the girl were also beautiful. Other admirers are falling by the wayside in scores. Caroline Dury was favoured before he left for Ripon and his examinations, though he may have already found the love of his life in Agnes Walton, who is nearby in Appleby. It appears that he is only faithful to the young lady nearest to him at the time. He sent us some dead birds shortly after the start of the season. At least Papa is pleased.

We have had visitors galore since June. Mary Taylor has been and gone, and as usual we enjoyed her company and her music. Then just lately cousin Branwell Williams and family came to visit (just for the day); they had been with Uncle Fennell at Cross-Stone. I wish you had been here — I found it impossible to talk to the daughter, Eliza, who is so 'religious' in that over-excited way, that I could get no sense out of her, and I tended to wander off to the kitchen and let Charlotte deal with her.

---

* Sarah Sugden is the eldest daughter of the late William Sugden, the wealthy Keighley manufacturer, and Mary Ann Greenwood (also deceased), the daughter of James Greenwood of Bridgehouse here in Haworth. Sarah is a very large woman. She has never married. The Sugden's home, Eastwood House, is the grandest house in Keighley.   Ed.

Write to me soon. I loved hearing about Scarbro' and the sea and the donkey ride. And I want to know more about these strange people called Robinson!

Your loving sister,
EJB

PS I forgot to say, Branwell has gone railway-mad. He has applied for a post with the new Leeds-Manchester Railway and has been told he will soon become the new assistant clerk at Sowerby Bridge. What do you think of that?!

I am alone again. The others are all gainfully employed; only I, the stay-at-home, am earning nothing. But I comfort myself with the knowledge that at least I am saving the family the cost of another servant. Martha is very willing but not always able. She does almost all the cleaning and some scullery work. I do the mending, ironing, and cooking. Aunt supervises. No, that isn't quite fair. She does sew a great deal, especially as we must provide new shirts for Branwell, and undergarments for Charlotte and Anne, who are both in employment. Charlotte's new position is with a family near Rawdon; she seems to be not too dissatisfied with it so far.

The Parsonage acquired a new resident last week: a beautiful young hawk. I found him struggling in a snare up on the moor above Ponden, his wing badly damaged. He was wild with fear as I untangled him (and I have the fierce bites and scratches to show for it), but he gradually calmed down after I wrapped him in my shawl. Mr. Wood found a cage for him and I hope he will recover sufficiently to be released back into his native wilderness. I call him Nero to please Papa.

I have made an important decision: it is time to end Gondal. I have started an epic poem in which Augusta is murdered. Let that be the final event. I want new characters, a new story, something stimulating and thrilling. I'm tired of being alone, of working to little purpose, tied to this house. Were it not for my daily excursions with Keeper, I think I should go mad. Aunt is ever cold and critical, Papa always in his study, writing letter after letter to the newspapers (and to what effect?). I visit Tabby as often as I can, but this is no substitute for having her all to myself in our kitchen.

EJB

So that was when she decided to end Gondal. First Queen Augusta, and then the Emperor Julius — dispatched within the year. In the summer of '41 we agreed to end these stories which had dominated our lives for so long. But I had wanted a complete termination of everything. Emily apparently only wanted a new story. I didn't understand then, but it is now clear that she desperately needed a creative arena for her boundless energies, and, as she was perforce required to stay at home, the fantasy world was the only one open to her at that time. And I admit my sin of envy; how I longed to be the one to remain at home. The death of little Mary Robinson that March affected me deeply; why is it that the innocent little babes seem to be the most frequent victims of Death's relentless harvest? As the happy years of my childhood slipped farther and farther away, and the grim realities of maturer years presented themselves, Haworth and home acquired an almost celestial glow in my mind. Well, it is useless to repine.

I did continue to wind up my part of the Chronicles, but my heart was not in it. Although life with the Robinsons was uncongenial yet it was also fascinating, and I had begun to think about using my experiences as a governess to write something for publication. But it was a long time before I undertook seriously to begin such an ambitious project. I was very lonely and often despairing while at Thorp Green, and my energies were completely used up in carrying out my duties.

AB

Emily and I were well aware of Anne's difficulties at Thorp Green but I had no idea that she was already considering the possibility of writing about it for publication. I wish we had confided in each other then. But Emily's wish for change is no surprise, and we soon found a way to satisfy it.

CB

Charlotte has just returned for the summer holidays from Upperwood House. Yesterday evening the family (except for Anne, who is at Scarbro', and Branwell who is fully employed at Luddenden Foot) met in conference, and we were quite astounded to be told that Charlotte's dream of our own school could become a reality! The suggestion came from Aunt Branwell, much to our surprise as she had never encouraged it before. Papa is less enthusiastic, but was outvoted. In any case, only Aunt has the capital to lift this project from idle daydreams into solid reality. But I am puzzled as to her motives. Has she at last given up all hope of any of us marrying? Or does she think that at least if we are all living away from home, she will be able to return to Penzance? Or perhaps she has decided that Uncle Fennell and his new wife need her more than Papa does (she has just gone to visit them at Cross-Stone this morning where he is very ill). Or, most likely, she simply wants to have Papa and the house to herself.

Whatever the reason, before she would be willing to advance the necessary funds, we must decide a host of details. Where should the school be situated? What accomplishments and subjects would we offer to our pupils? How many pupils, boarding or day? The list is very long. Charlotte will write to Anne this week about our plans; I'm sure she will be enthusiastic. As for myself, much as I would enjoy the three of us living together, I know I have little facility for educating young ladies. But I am happy to support the scheme — I am tired of living in the past and urgently need a plan for the future.

In the meantime, I have become more and more aware of the misery and suffering of some of the townsfolk, and the venality and mendacity of the mill owners. But I see no way of helping. No matter how the upcoming election turns out, I am quite sure that the 'lower orders' will not see any benefit. And Chartist agitation seems only to infuriate our manufacturers, so nothing is going to come of that.

However, some monies have been raised here to match

funds from London, and are to be put toward helping the most destitute (in the form of clothing, blankets, coal, etc.). Papa and I and the Church Wardens have been busy distributing these meagre supplies. But most wanting is food, and there is little to be had, and only at great expense. It is heart-breaking to see some of these poor families, crammed together, sometimes as many as twelve in a room, in which they cook, eat, sleep, and try to keep clean. The smell is asphyxiating, clean water a rarity, and now the pump is frozen, so they are reduced to using melted snow which is filthy with mud and soot. The children are like little skeletons, and their parents are not much better. Papa can hardly manage all the funerals he must perform.

And yet, amidst all the human suffering, the event which has touched me most is the death of our dear little cat, Tom. Strangely, his passing has brought back vivid feelings of grief, ones that I thought I would never feel again. Even Grasper's death did not affect me so deeply. It was several days before I could really believe it, and I kept looking for him, thinking I saw him everywhere. We buried him in the garden, under the black currant bushes. Even Papa was moved, and we prayed for his little soul in our evening prayers.

As for myself, I have lately found again some of my early delight in the beauty of the Earth which was a vital part of my life when I was young. Until a few months ago I had felt a great barrier between me and the natural world around me; I could see the beauty of it, but I could not enter into that deep sense of being a part of it. But since the beginning of summer, perhaps because of Tom Cat's death, I sometimes feel the coming of a great change in myself. Flashes of this change overwhelm me for brief moments when I seem to apprehend, with a larger awareness, the vastness of the universe, and I long to merge with that sublime spirit which pervades all time and space. Yesterday evening, just after sunset, I walked up to the top of our hill by the quarry, and stood for hours watching the stars appear, one by one. What a glorious sight! I could almost imagine myself being lifted up into the pure blue empyrean, and dissolving into it like a wisp of vapour. But these moments pass, and I become aware once more of our ugly, dirty world, and the hopeless suffering and degradation in our village. One would go mad dwelling on the injustice and inhumanity on this Earth, so in the end I generally sink back into my usual apathy, and get on with my chores.

EJB

The school plan had been through several incarnations by Christmas time and then had been suspended pending Emily and Charlotte's sojourn in Brussels. I own, I felt very left out, learning of that decision after it was made, and I was for a time rather bitter, may God forgive me. I felt so far away from home, adrift among strangers, more and more cut off from Emily. And she never wrote to me of the troubles in Haworth and her deep compassion for all those suffering mill folk. At Thorp Green all that was far away, and I rarely even saw a newspaper. Of course she had told me of Tom Cat's death, but she never confided to me how deeply it affected her. I wish she had.

AB

I know Anne was upset about the Brussels plan, but as I was still employed at Upperwood, it required all my free time to cope with the correspondence to and from the Continent and Haworth (where Papa and Aunt were both industrious in contacting their own acquaintance for advice about French and Belgian schools). I had to act expeditiously, and so, sadly, Anne often was the last to know of decisions which were often made (and unmade) very quickly.

CB

There have been several developments in the school plan. One of them is very humiliating to myself and Anne, but not surprising. Miss Wooler has offered her school at Dewsbury Moor to Charlotte. Charlotte was tempted at first but when Miss Wooler decreed that neither Anne nor I were to be a part of the school for the first six months, she quailed. Since then she has hatched another scheme, and a good one I think, in which she and I will spend a year at a good school on the Continent to perfect our French (mine is very rudimentary) and learn German. She rationalizes this as necessary accomplishments to attract pupils to our school (true) but I know she burns to see Europe and all its treasures, and I think she also wants to pry me loose from Haworth where she is convinced I am stagnating. Certainly she is right. Hard as it will be to exchange my accustomed freedom here for the restricted life of a school, it is time I bestirred myself and looked to the future. Charlotte, who is still at Upperwood House, is apparently constantly engaged in trying to find a suitable school for us, and has fixed on Brussels as her first choice. She has written to dozens of friends and acquaintances but has had no definite results as yet. But she has still not written to Anne about it, and has forbidden me to do so. This seems unusually cruel to me, and I intend to tell her the minute she arrives!

And she did! Charlotte was rather hurt, I think — after all, she was doing all the work of finding the school, making the arrangements. But they both thought that as I was so highly valued where I was placed, it was certainly desirable for me to remain there. Yet I still wish I could have gone abroad. If only we could have all undertaken this adventure together.

AB

I am quite convinced that I acted for the best for us all. Emily upbraided me at the time for not including Anne in all our decisions from the beginning, but, as she herself admits, I reasoned that there was no need as she already had a good position where she was greatly valued, so what would be the point? And in any case, it was just not practical. Also there was the question of her health, which was not hearty. Perhaps I have not done her justice, but once I had decided it was Emily who must receive some genuine formal education (Anne had had three years at Roe Head, Emily less than 3 months), I could not see any other way. We could not all three go to Brussels! When we finally wrote to Anne about our plan to spend a year, if possible, on the Continent, she seemed to understand, and not to be at all upset. It was only later that I learned she felt left out and misunderstood, and that she hated her post with the Robinsons, and would have relished a year abroad. But even if I had known, I would still have acted the same.

CB

This will be my last entry in this journal for some time; we leave for Brussels in a week. I intend to forego all temptation to neglect my studies. Poetry and fiction must be banished in favour of French essays and German grammar, and letters home must be concise (though, as Papa says, frequent). It will be a testing experiment in concentration.

Papa will accompany us, and we will be joined in Leeds by Mary Taylor and brother Joe for the first leg of our trip, the train journey up to London. Charlotte is in a fever of anticipation, and has made a long list of sights to see in the Metropolis. I am exhausted to think of all she wants to do. Oh, I must try to see this as a great adventure — it should certainly be interesting. After several days in the Capital, we sail for Ostend on the mail packet. Then we go by carriage to Brussels where Mary will leave us to join Martha at the Chateau de Koekelberg — a very elegant school near Brussels, and one which we could not afford. This will be more travelling than I have ever done in my life —

Farewell, England! Hail, Belgium!

EJB

———————————————

My plan to see as much as possible in London in a few short days was certainly ill-advised. I was dropping with weariness by the end of the first day. But Joe Taylor kept urging us on, and we did see some exhilarating sights. Mary and Emily and I disagreed on nearly everything, particularly some of the paintings in the beautiful new National Gallery, and so enjoyed ourselves immensely. But at least St Paul's inspired us all, though in different ways: I was deeply moved by the great tomb of Lord Nelson in the crypt; Emily was entranced by the magical properties of the whispering gallery under the Dome; and Mary drank in the entire scene — though her wry comment was, 'What a monument to Empire!' Papa was rather shocked by this which I think is what Mary intended.

I could write many pages on the events that followed — the trip to Brussels, the Pensionnat, M. and Mme. Heger — but this is Emily's story, and I decline to intrude my own tale of joy and woe.

CB

Enclosed between the next pages of the Journal were letters to us from Anne. Only one was in its envelope and is addressed, 'The Misses Charlotte and Emily Brontë, Chez Mde Heger-Parent, No. 32 Rue d'Isabelle, Bruxelle, Belgium. Care of Joseph Taylor, The Red House, Gomersal'.

Thorp Green
10 September, 1842

Dear Emily and Charlotte,

I have just had a short letter from Papa with the most tragic news — Mr. Weightman has died. * Branwell has also enclosed a detailed account of the death which has affected him deeply. W.W. will be greatly mourned and missed in the parish. I hope this reaches you before too long — unfortunately this will depend on Joe Taylor, and I have no knowledge of his next planned visit to Brussels. You have probably already received a letter from Papa or Branwell with the same intelligence, but I wanted to add my voice to theirs as I know you both were very fond of him. Oh, I wish we were all at home together.*

All my love and sympathy,

Anne

Haworth
25 October, 1842

Dear Emily and Charlotte,

Again I am the bearer of bad news. Aunt is very ill. I am not certain of the cause, but she is in great pain, and Papa says that there is little hope of her surviving, and wishes you both to come home as quickly as possible. I was given leave to return to Haworth and am now at home. I beg you to hurry.

All my best love,

---

* Dear William Weightman died on the 6 September, 1842, aged only 28.   Ed.

Anne
Haworth
29 October 1842

Dear Emily and Charlotte,

Aunt Branwell breathed her last sometime early this morning. We are all grateful that her suffering is over. God grant her peace and rest — she had a sad life with much shade and little sunshine. The funeral is the first of November. I know you cannot arrange to be with us for the service and interment, but please come as soon as you can. Branwell is devastated and Papa seems confused and distracted. I long to see you.

Your loving sister,

Anne

How very strange it is to read over one's own letters. Even my handwriting appears alien. But I remember in vivid detail the few weeks which elapsed between Aunt's death and my return to Thorp Green. For me it was a mixture of happiness at my sisters' return, but mainly great sadness at the deaths of Aunt, Mr. Weightman, and Martha Taylor. Papa and Branwell were the most affected by Aunt's death, though Branwell was, for once, able to look to the future with optimism as an agreement was soon reached with the Robinsons that he would be employed as young Edmund's tutor. Charlotte's account of Martha's demise at the Chateau de Koekelberg, which she learned from Mary Taylor, was very moving if rather short on facts. She and Emily and Mary left flowers on Martha's grave in the Protestant cemetery in Brussels. But I think that it was the death of W.W. which caused us all the most pain. In a way every one of us loved him — he had so much promise and died so young.

I was called back to Thorp Green at the end of November, and it was one of the most heart-rending partings I have ever endured.

AB

November, 1842

What a great gulf there seems between my last entry in this Journal and this, my first, since returning home. I can at least say in these pages that I feel no great sorrow for Aunt's death. Charlotte admits she feels the same. Anne, on the other hand, was always Aunt's favourite niece, and feels her loss deeply. Branwell is profoundly saddened — this is natural — he looked on her almost as his mother. I feel nothing but liberation. And now we each will have some capital to spend or invest as we like.*

The death of William Weightman is another matter. He was a bright and cheering presence in our otherwise dull lives, and we will all miss him greatly — particularly poor Papa who is now without any support in both Church and Civil affairs. I hope I can fill the void.

Yet I am very happy to be at home again. Our homecoming, though sad, was much brightened by the advent of a new puppy — Anne was given a little King Charles Spaniel by the Robinsons in a touching gesture of consolation, and she brought it home with her. The puppy is to be called Flossey, and she is a lively and lovable little creature. Anne has asked me to look after her, and teach her good manners.

Charlotte is trying to persuade me to return to Brussels with her, but I plan to dig in my heels and stay put. Papa now needs me here more than ever before. And for myself, although I am pleased to have learned French and a smattering of German, and I am grateful to M. Heger for the opportunity to write prose to some purpose, and for his discipline — even when I resented his approach to composition — now I wish to write without his dark presence hovering over me.

On the whole, the time spent in Brussels has done me good. My French is now serviceable, and I am making strides in German. Also, I was able to improve my skills as a

---

* Aunt Branwell left her four nieces (myself, Emily, and Anne, and Eliza Kingston in Penzance) each the sum of £300.   Ed.

pianist, and have come home with instructions from my teacher à Bruxelles to keep up my exercises as well as to improve my sight-reading. Before I left he insisted on giving me two books by that devilish tormentor of the young, Czerny. But as a teacher of the piano to others, I fear I will never have the knack of inspiring pupils. My little beginners at the Pensionnat were all quite resentful when I insisted that they must give up their free time for their lessons, and not impinge on my own precious hours of leisure. My experience at Law Hill had taught me that, at least. But I was unable to recover their good opinion no matter how encouraging I was with their lamentable efforts. But there was one girl who responded well to my teaching — Mlle. Louise de Bassompierre. This was because she was already very accomplished at the piano. We often played duets together to our mutual satisfaction and enjoyment. I gave her one of my sketches when I left, and she has promised to write to me.

A great deal has taken place here since February last. Haworth is in an even sorrier state than when I left —with the increasingly severe downturn in trade and the rise of the 'mob', as Papa would say. Poor souls, without work or bread, and with only a poor relief system designed to put them in the workhouse. There is much talk of riot and revolution, even here in Haworth. And the owners of the mills are much affected by bad trade and the general atmosphere of anxiety and strife. There has been one suicide already, and I fear the future holds a dreary fate for many others.

As for family events, the worst by far is that Branwell was dismissed for negligence from his position with the Leeds & Manchester Railway. He is suitably contrite, but for him the real tragedy is that he is somewhat cut off from a new circle of very interesting friends. He seems unsure as to what path he will now follow, but his ambition to be a published author is stronger than ever. He has had many poems published in the local newspapers over the past year, and has had much encouragement from various men (and women) of letters to whom he has sent specimens of his work. But can he earn his living in this way, I wonder?

103

There is some talk that the Robinsons are looking for a tutor for their son, and Anne has written to them, suggesting Branwell's appointment to the post. I hope this plan bears fruit — the thought of the two of them working together, perhaps displaying their musical talents for their employers' family and guests, is a pretty picture indeed.

EJB

Branwell joined me at Thorp Green at the end of January. If only I had known then what the future held, I would have told him to turn about and go straight home! But at first the arrangement seemed ideal, and he was very popular both with the children and their parents. And when he arrived, the house and grounds looked especially beautiful, under a great white expanse of snow — he was in seventh heaven. He said it was far superior to the Postlethwaites.

AB

Because I knew I would be returning to Brussels in the new year, I was not as down-hearted as Anne or Branwell. Emily, bless her, was a support to us all with her cheerful good sense and unfailing humour. I think she was genuinely pleased to be mistress of the house. I was also greatly cheered by an exchange of visits with Ellen; together we shared memories of Martha Taylor, and this lightened our burden of grief. Aunt's death, on the other hand, as Emily rightly remarked, hardly touched me. I know we owed her much, but I was never, in all that time that she lived with us, able to feel anything more for her than grudging respect. But the loss of William W. shocked and saddened us all. Branwell was quite overwhelmed by his death and Aunt's, both of which he witnessed. Poor lad. At that time I was able to feel great sympathy for him — he was like a cripple whose two crutches had been suddenly kicked away. But worse was to follow.

CB

105

Before we went away I had thought I would finish with Gondal. I had allowed all the major characters to die or be killed, but while in Brussels the temptation to at least dwell on the Gondalian past was too great and I succumbed. Now I fear I may never escape this terrible desire to return to the world which Anne and I and Robert and John created over ten years ago. Anne seems to have given up on Gondal for the moment; well, she was never as committed as I — she has moved on. After all, she has a new life, which, though difficult, is leading her away from Gondal and from me.

Life here at home is very quiet. The monotony of the days is only enlivened by the excitement of a letter from Anne or Branwell. We no longer have my hawk, Nero, nor the geese. I suspect Aunt disposed of them as soon as I left. Keeper and Flossy are good company, but our conversations are rather one-sided. And Papa and I are very solitary creatures at best. Though we discuss at breakfast his many problems in the Parish, and I play the piano or read to him after tea, he prefers to be alone in his study most of the day, just as I prefer to walk out on the moors (weather permitting) with only the dogs for company. But I think Papa misses Aunt more than he would be willing to admit. They used to argue cheerfully for hours on end about politics and religion and such like. I fear I would only lose my temper (or cause him to lose his) so we avoid any subject which might result in an argument. But I have persuaded him, as tactfully as possible, to give up evening prayers. And I think he sees the sense in this.

At least our faithful Tabby has returned to us at last, and often, after Papa has gone up to bed, I spend the evening in the kitchen with her, listening to her tales of Haworth in the old days. Yet I begin to wonder if anything of interest will ever happen to me. The school plan seems more distant than ever.

I have been studying the newspapers to learn more about our new railway shares, and have decided, in spite of Branwell's unhappy experience with the Leeds &

Manchester, to leave the money, which Aunt had already invested, where it is, and perhaps acquire a few more shares. Charlotte and Anne agree and have given me carte blanche to act on their behalf in the matter of buying and selling if necessary. The York & North Midland Railway looks, indeed, most promising — I think Mr. Hudson has the vision and the nerve to maintain his already spectacular success. Aunt was very shrewd in money matters, if not in other ways.

EJB

How grateful we were that Emily volunteered to deal with Aunt's bequests. Branwell was rather cross that Aunt had not left him any cash, and refused to advise us on anything, and Papa, as usual, left the decisions to us. He, too, was surprised that Aunt had not included him as a legatee, not even of any personal possessions (at least Branwell was willed a keepsake), but he was philosophical, and said that it was right to take care of the next generation, and in any case he did not expect to outlive Aunt by many years, so what would have been the point.

AB

Yes, Papa was always reminding us that he would not live forever, and that we must all be able to support ourselves in the event of his death. Now it appears that he will probably outlive us all. With four of his six children already in the grave, and the likelihood that Anne and I will follow ere long, he must wonder at the inscrutable ways of a God who takes the young before the old. I certainly do.

CB

The past month has been surprisingly eventful. Who would have thought that both local and great national events would affect my own life so directly!

In February Papa was made aware by Joseph Greenwood, Esq., that a forged document had been registered at Wakefield the previous year, transferring the Buttergate Sykes estate from old John Beaver to his son James. Now we all knew that Mr. Beaver had disinherited his son (in favour of his two granddaughters) about five years ago because of his scandalous relationship with Susie Farrar (Papa had witnessed the will), so this was both a crime and a scandal. Mr. Greenwood and three other magistrates looked into the matter, and decided criminal charges were in order. John Farrar and Will Marsh, who colluded in the forgery, were taken into custody and sent to York — and James Beaver was charged, but couldn't be found. He later gave himself up, almost certainly because he had made a deal with the prosecutor. So at the beginning of last month, Papa, Mr. Greenwood, and Mr. Thomas (who is an executor of John Beaver's will, and is the father-in-law of one of Mr. Beaver's granddaughters) all went to York for the Assizes as witnesses for the prosecution. They were duly sworn in, but they were never called to testify! It seems that James privately admitted his crime, gave up all claim to his father's property, and the judge simply let the case collapse when the prosecution presented no evidence. And to cap it all, poor old John Beaver died the very day of the trial. I suppose all's well that ends well, but I truly think that Mr. James was very lucky indeed, and as for that Susie Farrar, I suspect she was behind the whole thing. James was so smitten with her, he would have done almost anything for her.

Now, the way in which all this affected me is this: when Papa and Mr. Greenwood and Mr. Thomas went to York, they left Haworth in a potentially dangerous condition. The leaders of the riots of last August were being tried at that very time at the Lancaster Assizes, so there were rumblings all over the West Riding that further disturbances were planned to coincide with the trials.[*] To leave Haworth thus with no clerical or civil authority in place (not the Minister, nor the Magistrate, nor the Chairman of the Vestry) was rather risky — accordingly the Vestry met and swore in 50 special constables to keep an eye on things. And I was left in charge of the Parsonage, aided by Tabby and Martha and Keeper. But Papa was anxious and afraid of what might happen if the physical force Chartists and their hangers-on decided to take advantage of the undefended Parsonage. He was clearly remembering the stirring times of the Luddites when he began his habit of carrying a loaded pistol, and consequently he decided that I must learn to shoot! I must be able to defend the household! Well, to soothe his agitation, I agreed, even though I knew full well that no one would dare attack the Parsonage with Tabby in full voice and Keeper straining at the lead. And I also knew that I would never be able to fire the pistol at any living creature, unless under imminent threat. But to placate him I did as he instructed, and became a reasonably good shot, and he entrusted me with one of his two pistols.

In the end there was not and has not been any serious uprising in Haworth. But I did have to deal with some poor folk, who, knowing I was in sole command of the Parsonage, and thinking I would be more generous than Tabby and Papa, came early one morning to the door, begging for food and any cast-off clothing. I gave them as much as we could spare — several pounds of oatmeal and wheat flour, a ham, and a sack of potatoes, and a pile of Papa and Branwell's old shirts. They seemed very grateful and well-behaved, and left quietly, promising no further disturbance. Tabby was very cross with me for giving away our precious stores, but I told her, it is a small price to pay for peace, and these folk are far

---

[*] The riots of the 14th to the 18th of August, 1842, to which Emily refers, are now generally known as the Plug Riots: thousands of unemployed factory operatives marched from Lancashire into Yorkshire, removing the plugs from the boilers of the steam-powered spinning factories on their way. All the villages near Bradford were affected, including Haworth, though the rioters were dispersed by the militia before they could enter Bradford.   Ed.

more needy than we. Yet Tabby was right after all — two days later, some of the same people returned, this time with reinforcements; they <u>demanded</u> more food, and now they wanted blankets as well. Their manner had entirely changed. It was a salutary lesson in human nature. I told them we had no more that we could spare, and that they should apply to the Poor Law Guardians. This only made them more angry, saying in effect 'so much for Christian Charity when even the Parson's wealthy family refuses to help the poor and destitute'. Of course their language was a good deal more colourful than that. Then they started to move toward me, flourishing their pitchforks. At this point I waved my pistol at them and fired over their heads, and Tabby shouted out, 'Get ye away from here, ye ungrateful wretches! Just wait till t' Parson comes home, and hears that ye have threatened his daughter!' Then Keeper started growling, straining at his lead, and at that they scurried away like frightened rabbits. It was a scene I shall never forget.

Papa is at home again now, thank God. While he was in York and waiting for the trial to commence, he paid a visit to Anne and Branwell at Thorp Green. He was very pleased with their situation and with the great warmth and respect with which they are treated by Mr. and Mrs. Robinson, and by the children.

We finally have a new curate to replace W. W., who is now even more sadly missed than before. The new man, Mr. Smith, is a revolting creature — bigoted and opinionated. He arrived only a few days before Papa went to York, and has been antagonizing the townsfolk at every opportunity. Why they don't rise up and turn him out at once can only be explained by their fear that open rebellion might end in bloodshed. Papa doesn't like him but needs his help, so we will have to tolerate the man until Papa can find a replacement or until he decides to move on.

I have started on some new Gondal stories, but find them unsatisfying. I keep wanting to revert to the old ones. Will this bond to the days of my youth ever release me? I have spent most of my time revising the poems begun in Brussels.

111

One other event of particular interest, at least to me, although so far it has not affected me directly — the Clayton family has moved back to Haworth. Old Nathan was unable to make a go of it in Denholme, where they decamped immediately after Robert's death, and thanks to the Greenwoods (how ironic) he is now the new toll keeper for the Blue Bell Trust, and lives up on the Brow with his remaining family. They also have a farm of sorts up there. I wrote them several letters after Robert died, but had no answers. I am reluctant to visit them, but feel that I must, and before too long.

EJB

This entry is so interesting, and such a surprise. I knew Emily was alone with the servants in the Parsonage while Papa was in York, and I knew that she had been taught to handle a pistol, but to actually use it? It seems completely against her nature. How little we ever know even those closest to us. At any rate, this entry explains why Papa was particularly proud of her after that time, and was always calling her his 'own dear brave girl'.

AB

Emily wrote to me of some of these events while I was in Brussels, but I, like Anne, had no idea of what a stirring time it must have been for her. I had already decided to base one of the heroines of my current novel on Emily's forthrightness and independence of spirit, and this affirms how correct I am to do so. But now I shall also try to incorporate her great concern for the poor folk suffering about her. How glad Emily would have been to have had huge wealth to devote to charity, and I've no doubt she would have been thoroughly sensible and organized in deciding how to administer it. She was always eminently practical, at least where others were concerned. I'm sure she would have found a way of overcoming the deplorable human tendency to resent charity, and of distributing it without the loss of the recipients' self-respect.

As for Anne's remark that it was not in Emily's nature to actually use a pistol, I fear this is far from true; Emily had a violent streak in her which rose to the surface whenever she was provoked. I must remind Anne of the time Emily punished Keeper for sleeping on her bed and pummelled his face mercilessly until the blood ran. And once, when she discovered Branwell teasing Grasper by tempting him with a bit of mutton, then snatching it away, she flew into a rage, grabbed the meat and threw it across the garden, and then smashed B in the face with her fist, saying 'Branwell, you brute! How would you like Tabby to remove your chop before you'd eaten it?' No human being was safe from her wrath if he teased or threatened a dumb beast in her presence, but no animal was to be permitted to disobey her.

CB

113

We have just entertained Dr. Scoresby at tea today. He was visiting Papa to discuss the new school and stayed on until the evening. Though he has visited us before, this is the first time that I was to be hostess for the event. He is a fascinating man, knows extraordinary things, has done so much to excite one's interest and curiosity. I told him about our early interest in the subject of Arctic exploration, and how thrilled we were to read about Ross and Parry when we were children. He was somewhat subdued by my enthusiasm and then explained that he still felt some bitterness about the first Ross and Parry expedition. He was, at that time, the most experienced and knowledgeable Arctic explorer in the country, and was thought by many to be the logical candidate to lead the search for the Northwest Passage. But, as he confided to us, the secretary to the Admiralty, Mr. Barrow, had taken a strong dislike to him, and he was ignored, probably because he was not a naval man. I was very embarrassed — I had forgotten that there had once been much support for Dr. Scoresby to captain that expedition. Even Blackwood's Magazine had supported him. There was an awkward silence... Fortunately, at that point Martha came in to clear away, so we went on to other topics.

There is something compelling about Dr. Scoresby — he is very fierce in appearance, dark and rather intimidating — his eyes fix one with an almost mesmeric gaze, and it is very hard to look away.

A few months ago I finally found the courage to climb the hill to Brow Top Farm, the new home of Nathan and Sally Clayton. Sally was in the kitchen with the baby, Mary Ann. Needless to say, she was very surprised to see me, but she washed her hands (they were bloody from butchering a rabbit), and bade me sit down. We exchanged a few laconic words about the weather, and then there was a very uncomfortable silence. Finally I blurted out, 'So, did you ever receive those letters I sent you at Trough Bottom?' She blushed and looked away, and then admitted to me that she couldn't read, but she knew those letters were from me (because John Brown had delivered them for me), and she didn't want her husband to see them, as he was still very upset and angry about Robert's death, and appeared to think that I was the cause. This was disturbing news — it somehow had never occurred to me that he, a good Quaker, would be angry with _me_! But before I could respond, she had gone to a cupboard and taken out a thin packet of letters from behind a large mixing bowl. 'Nathan knows nowt of t' letters, and he must nae. But would ye be so kind, and read me one of 'em?' They were all still sealed. So, with trembling hands, I took the earliest one from the little group and unsealed it. It was a strange feeling to open this missive, the first I had written after Robert's death. I quote, as best I can, from memory. 'Dear Mr. and Mrs. Clayton, I take up my pen to send you a few words of heartfelt sympathy for the loss of your dear son, Robert. His death, surely by a tragic accident, was a stunning blow to us all here at the Parsonage, and I know that you, his loving parents, must be heart-broken. If I can be of service to you in any way, I hope you will call on me. Yours in deep sorrow, Emily Jane Brontë'. Sally stood quietly while I was reading, her tears falling unnoticed. 'Oh, Miss Em'ly,' she said, 'that war reight beautiful. Are they all like that?' As far as I could remember, they were. Then she said she would show them to her husband that very day, and she hoped he could now find it in his heart to forgive me. I asked her if he really thought I was responsible for Robert's death, and she said he certainly did at the time — 'The poor lad war that cut up over you steppin' out with Master Greenwood, he told his dad that he might run away to sea. After that Nathan took agin ye somethin' flaysome, and when our boy was found on t' moor, frozen stiff, he said we mun flit at once and not bide one more week in Stanbury. I'm sorry...' My faced burned, and I stammered out something like an apology. Then she asked me the question I knew must be asked — did I ever love her son, and if I did, why did I treat him so badly? So we sat and talked for over an hour, and I tried to explain my confusion and childishness at that time, and to assure her that I would never have married James Greenwood, that it was all a

115

trivial flirtation of which I am heartily ashamed. As to my feelings for Robert, I found it quite impossible to convey to her how deep was my love for him, and how his death had changed my life for ever. But I think at least she grasped that for me his death was a great loss, and a genuine source of true sorrow. And then I asked her my own difficult question — if I had accepted Robert's proposal of marriage (that is, if Papa had let me), would she and her husband have been pleased or unhappy. She looked at me amazed. Apparently the possibility had never crossed her mind. In fact she never even knew that Robert had asked me! I decided to leave her in ignorance of my misbegotten plan to ask Robert to leave home and seek success in the world. And after asking about other matters (her family, the farm, etc.) I took my leave. I think she now has a better opinion of me than before, and I hope she can persuade her husband that I am not the heartless jade he thought I was.

EJB

Well, one surprise after another! I never knew that Emily had had anything to do with the Claytons after Robert's death. How very brave of her to visit them; but how strange that she never told me. And as for her reaction to Dr. Scoresby, do I detect his shadow behind the character of Heathcliff?

AB

Indeed this entire entry is a surprise — she never said anything to me about Dr. Scoresby other than a description of his troubles in the Parish, which were legion. I had no idea she found him so attractive, so fascinating! Her visit to the Clayton home, however, even though I knew nothing of it, seems entirely in character. Emily never refused to face an unpleasant duty.

CB

Anne and Branwell have just returned to Thorp Green. We had a wonderful Christmas, and they were at home long enough to greet Charlotte on her eagerly-awaited return from Brussels. Now Charlotte and I rule the roost, much to my, Tabby's, and Martha's satisfaction. Charlotte is a wonder at cleaning and sewing, and this allows me to devote more time to my writing. And, of course, to the piano. The music I brought back from Brussels, though it is merely some difficult exercises, has been a great challenge. It is time that I acquire some new pieces.

But Charlotte is not happy to be home again. This comes as no surprise, though she admits that she was very miserable in Brussels for a long time before she came home. She confided to me that her regard for M. Heger was beginning to be more a source of suffering than of pleasure. I hope that time will heal her pain.

I have persevered with the new Gondal stories but it is a struggle; I may have to revert to the old ones. Poor Augusta may have to be resurrected.

EJB

More than time was required to 'heal my pain'. Emily never fully realized that my feelings for my Master were too deep to be healed by the passage of time. I think I have never fully recovered from those wounds. But the only cure of any efficacy is ACTION, which I soon learned.

CB

This is a vexatious time indeed. Although I am content with my own lot, I begin to be annoyed with everyone else. These hard times call forth the worst in the human character. Mr. Smith rants on about the need for the labouring classes to accept their lot of suffering and to do nothing about it but look forward to their 'eternal reward'. Oh, it makes me so angry! But on the other hand, the physical force Chartists are girding their loins for serious confrontation, which is only going to exacerbate the situation, and lead the mill owners to resort to calling in the militia yet again. What can be done? I see no way to help, except by offering charity to the poor, and even that is often resented, or worse, repulsed.

And at home Charlotte continues moody and depressed — I persuade her to walk out on the moors with me as often as possible, but she hasn't the stamina to go very far. She is constantly expecting a letter from M. Heger, and writes to him far too often — it has become an obsession. Another sign of this obsession, I believe, is her increasing tendency to be over-tidy, and to criticise me for my slovenly ways. If I see her rearrange her desk box once more, I shall scream. Even Tabby has started to complain that Charlotte interferes in her kitchen arrangements, reorganizing the cupboards, washing up dishes that Tabby has already washed and dried. I know Tabby is not quite as fastidious as formerly, but she is very sensitive to these implied criticisms. On the other hand, I am loath to reproach Charlotte — I can see she needs to have control over some portion of her life, and if cleaning and tidying help her through this difficult time, so be it. I only wish she would not fix me with her 'basilisk stare' when I forget to put away my papers!

Papa's eyes are becoming weaker, and so he is rather querulous. He needs help with both reading and writing, and is constantly either complaining that he gets no help, or apologising for being a nuisance. Something will have to be done, but what?

To soothe my agitation, I have begun to transcribe my better verses into two notebooks, one for Gondal and one for my personal effusions. It is a strange experience. Some are so bad I wonder I ever saved them, and they will not go in. Still I cannot bring myself to the point of burning them — my little misbegotten, ill-favoured children. But others are better than I remembered, and with a little polishing I think they are nothing to be ashamed of.

EJB

Those years (1844 – 45) may have been the worst of my entire life. Not only was I in the depths of despair over the separation from my Master, and the constantly dashed hopes of at least receiving the occasional letter from him, but eventually even Emily lost patience with me, and I could no longer confide in her. I was well aware that she found my obsession with cleanliness irritating and I admit I was equally irritated by her carelessness. It could not be helped — I was barely in control of my emotions, and it took an iron will not to lash out at everyone or even, on one occasion, to throw myself into the River Worth; at least the mindless duties of household cleaning generally kept me from thoughts of self-harm. Well, Emily had had over seven years to recover from her personal tragedy, and in any case at least Robert's death was final, while I suffered the knowledge that M. Heger yet lived, but no longer wished to know me. Nevertheless, her unspoken criticism had its effect; it was about that time that I revived the school project.

CB

The entire household is in mourning. Tiger, our darling little cat, died of a short illness two days ago. He was only three years old. We have buried him next to Tom in the garden. It moves me to tears even to think of him, such a playful, mischievous little creature. He had a happy life, though short, but I think we will not have another cat — the pain of losing them is too great.

Charlotte has been and come back from Ellen's — she desperately needed this break, and so did we. She seems more at ease now, but it may be only temporary. Ellen has thoughtfully sent me some flower seeds which must wait a few months before sowing. She says she may visit us in the summer, and for Charlotte's sake, I hope she will.

Charlotte has a new plan. I am not sure that it will ever see
the light of day, but at least she is forcing herself to think
about the future. The new plan is to set up our school here in
the Parsonage. There are many reasons why this is not a
promising idea, but I have bitten my tongue, and given her
my support. Happily, Anne has been included in the scheme
from the beginning this time, and she is willing to do her
part, though I think she, too, has reservations as to the
likelihood of success. But I did make it very clear to both of
them that the burden of teaching must descend on their
shoulders — I am a hopeless instructress, and have come to
actively dislike young girls as a species. However, it is
probably essential that music be offered as an extra, and
Charlotte has persuaded me that I must make this an
exception, so I have agreed to teach the piano to any pupils
who are truly serious and willing to practise. Otherwise, it is
agreed that I will attend to the physical requirements of the
school, — the housekeeping, the dietary, etc. But I think
Charlotte has not realized what the real obstacle to this plan
will be, and that is Papa. Of course, he now says he is quite
willing to share the house with half a dozen lasses, as well as
Tabby and Martha and the three of us. No, I see no way to
make this house large enough to accommodate a school and
a septuagenarian (almost) who loves his peace and quiet.

I, however, have lately begun to long for a real
undertaking of my own. This feeling crystallized late last
evening, and I have not spoken yet to anyone about it, not
even Anne. I was sitting late in the garden as twilight
gathered 'round me, with my box on my lap, thinking about
a new poem. I had been angry all day long, with Charlotte
and with Papa — there is so much suffering in the village
and Charlotte seems unaware of it. Papa spends his time
writing angry letters to the newspapers, on many subjects
which arouse his wrath, but what effect does this have on the
immediate and urgent situation here in Haworth? I, too,
wanted to write something angry and defiant, but that seems
to be so pointless — my poems are not going to make life

better for any except myself. And then the thought entered my head, why not write something to be read by others? Why not write a novel, something to rouse the apathetic reader to take action, and cure the malaise of the labouring classes and the greed of the manufacturers? But I immediately dismissed that thought as too impossibly ambitious to be a practical undertaking, and in any case, it would be of no more use than Papa's endless letters to the Intelligencer. But the idea of writing for publication would not go away, and I feel strangely drawn to write a work of fiction for publication. I have no clear idea of what my 'book' will be about, but I think it will have to reflect my own experience of life. I must speak to Anne about this.

Now, I must record a fascinating dream I had the other day. I dreamt it was springtime, and I was walking out on the moors; I was wrapped in deep depression, and felt completely shut out from the beauty all around me. I lay down on the heath. Then suddenly I heard the most beautiful music — it came from everywhere at once, and I saw many tiny shining silver harps being played by invisible hands. And I felt such a wave of joy and hope as I had never felt since Robert died. When I awoke the feeling continued, and for a time at least, I was so sure that Robert and I would meet again. It probably means nothing, but on the other hand, who can say?

EJB

_____

Emily and I conferred briefly on the matter of novel-writing while I was at home in June. At that point Charlotte was much engrossed with ideas and plans for our 'school', so we just let her get on with it, and kept these early ideas for novels to ourselves. In any case, neither of us had any clear idea of what we would write, though I had been thinking about it in a general way for some time.

AB

I suppose the school idea really was unrealistic, and it was almost a relief finally to give it up. But at that time it was at least something concrete and hopeful to think about; all the practicalities and problems were very absorbing. But I wish they had included me in their thoughts about writing for publication — it might have made our later disputes over publishing our poetry much less distressing.

CB

Anne and Branwell are now at Scarborough with the Robinsons. Before they left, Anne and I had a serious talk about the Gondal Chronicles, and also about other writing. She would like to give up Gondal, but I am not quite ready to do so; since she left I have busied myself in writing a life of the Emperor Julius Brenzaida. But we both feel that we might have more to say about the real world than we have done. I must own that writing Gondal is a pleasant and engrossing pastime, but, after all, it was never more than a game. Anne is seriously thinking of writing, in story form, a book about her time as governess with the Inghams and the Robinsons, but with a happy ending. I hope she can do it. I, sadly, have only one story to write, and it could never have a happy ending unless I completely invented it. Well, I suppose I could do that. It might be interesting to imagine the various ways in which my story might have turned out had Robert not died. Suppose I had married James, but Robert had not died, and had only left the area. Suppose he returned, rich and educated, as I wanted him to do. What would have happened then? Or suppose that I had married James, and then he had died. Would I have married Robert? There are so many possibilities, this is going to require a great deal of thought. But I think the central theme must reflect my great quandary during that brief period when I was torn between James and Robert. Then, with Robert's death, the decision was taken out of my hands. Oh, it torments me still. How could I have been so selfish and stupid not to realize the suffering of which I was the cause? By the time I understood my own feelings it was too late — Robert was dead. Dead. Oh, stop this, Emily Jane — think about something else.

Ellen Nussey came for her promised visit earlier this month. It was a pleasant change for us, and as we were all briefly at home at that time, the house was crowded and bustling and full of 'mirth and jollity'. Ellen's visit came hard on the heels of the birth of Flossy's first litter of puppies (only three of which survived) so she was presented by Papa with her pick of the litter. I fear we will not be able to keep the other two as Keeper has taken a distinct dislike to them. As he is their father, I was shocked at his unpaternal behaviour, but he is a dog, after all, and even some humans are known to dislike their offspring to the point of harming them. So we hope to find homes for both of them where I trust they will be well-loved and cared for.

EJB

Poor Ellen didn't know what we were imposing upon her by the gift of Flossy Junior — she was even more mischievous than her mother. But Ellen was very fond of her, and Flossy Jr did learn more mannerly ways eventually.

Emily must be right about our discussions regarding our writing — I really don't remember our conversations then being so specific. However, Agnes Grey was in my mind for such a long time before I started to write, that it is very hard to remember what stage it had reached when I first discussed it with Emily. And I'm sure we never talked about her ideas for her book — she never confided such personal thoughts to me any more. But it is gratifying to learn that she had begun at last to be able to think about all those terrible events in a calm and ordered frame of mind.

AB

I wish I could have done the same. I still hope that some day I will, but that time has not yet arrived.

CB

At last, Mr. Smith has left us! This is a blessing for Papa, even though as a result he requires my constant help as he is almost completely blind. With Dr. Scoresby's help (and insistence) he has succeeded in finding a new curate, and I think that young Mr. Grant will be acceptable. However, since most of his time is taken up with the Grammar School, Papa still needs more help here in the village. So I still read and write his letters for him, and Charlotte and I read to him every evening before he goes to bed. We have been reading episodes of a new novel serialised in Fraser's by a very clever writer, Mr. Thackeray (who uses the ridiculous pen name of Fitzboodle!) — it is called The Luck of Barry Lyndon.

We have decided to give up the school project — for the simple reason that we could not find any pupils willing to enrol in our school. I am greatly relieved by this turn of events, and Charlotte is not as disappointed as I had expected. Our monies are safely invested and give us a good return, so we needn't be concerned about our finances at least for the moment.

EJB

Had it not been for Branwell I would have been tempted to give up my position at this time — we could now afford for me to come home for an extended period, and the Robinson girls were certainly old enough to no longer need governessing. But I was growing uneasy about Branwell's health — he seemed always to be suffering from a bad cough and low fever, and he had several fits in which he fell to the ground and lost consciousness for several minutes. But more worrying even than his health was his behaviour with Mrs. R., which was beginning to be openly affectionate. I feared at any moment he might be discovered and I tried to persuade him that we must leave or he must moderate his behaviour, but he only laughed at me, and said I could leave if I wanted to but wild horses could not drag him away. So, of course, I had to stay. As it turned out it would only be a little over half a year before I was at home again for good, and Branwell's indiscretions caused his dismissal. Little did we know at that time what Fate had in store for us.

AB

The collapse of the school enterprise was, as Emily says, a relief, particularly for Papa. I was sorry then not to have been more successful, but now I see that it was for the best — it spurred us on to better things.

CB

131

Christmas is past; it was a very productive time for Anne and me. I have been writing some verse, and am at work on the final volume of the First Wars. Anne was very despondent when she arrived home for the holidays, but we plunged back into Gondal and she now seems rather more cheerful. We finally are beginning a new phase of our saga, with a new generation of characters, though this is still only in the playing stage (nothing written yet). But before we say farewell to the old ones, we are recording their history in an orderly way, and we have both written several poems recalling them and all their tragedies and troubles. I even succumbed to my old memories of those happy years when Robert was still the most important person in my life, and I rewrote the Death of Alexander Elbë (Robert).* It is better than the first one, though perhaps not as deeply felt. Anne and I no longer always share all our poetry.

But we all appear to be entertaining similar thoughts about writing more serious prose works. Branwell has been sending his work to various eminent authors for their opinions, and has received some encouragement. Anne and I have not been so ambitious, and in any case, the opinion of others (outside the family circle) would only be a burden for me — I would feel strange eyes peering over my shoulder, cold and critical, and I would never be able to write a line.

Branwell seems to think that writing a novel will be terribly easy, and has already written a few chapters. He may be right that for him it is easy, but that is because he has no high ambitions to make it good! There is something unsettling in his behaviour — we all noticed it over the holidays. He seemed at first buoyant, yet rather nervous, and would then suddenly become overwhelmed with depression and guilt, the cause of which we can only guess. Anne told me that Branwell is very highly thought of at Thorp Green,

---

* This poem, to which I referred earlier, is Emily's last account of the death of Alexander Elbë. It is dated the 2 December, 1844. We revised it for publication under the title, 'A Death Scene'.   Ed.

but she fears that Mrs. Robinson appears to be rather over-fond of him, and is always telling Anne what a paragon her brother is. We all know how susceptible Branwell is to flattery.

really?

But to return to the plans for novels. Charlotte, who is still very despondent over M. Heger, who almost never writes to her, may try to write something of her Brussels experience. She thinks she may disguise it by having the protagonist be a man, and not very sympathetic. I think this is a very bad idea — first of all because it won't then be her own story in any meaningful way, and secondly, because she is still in a turmoil over what happened there. Still, she may benefit from having a serious new project to tackle now that the school plan has been given up; and at the very least it may take her mind off the arrival of the post each morning.

Anne has laudably modest ambitions for her book, which I am sure will be as straightforward and healthful as herself. It may not be a great stirring tale, but I am sure it will be pleasingly written and it will be truthful.

As for me, I am beginning to form some picture in my mind of what I would like to write. Branwell and I have discussed this at some length; he has some interesting ideas. But the core of the story is all mine, partially reflecting my dilemma over Robert and James. It will be based on two love triangles. My vision is to present a vast, spiritual love that ends in tragedy, and a lesser, more mundane love that ends happily. In the first, the heroine dies and her lovers survive in hatred; in the second, which will be connected to the first, the weaker of the two lovers dies, and the second heroine can marry the other lover and live happily ever after. I am rather pleased with the almost geometric symmetry of the arrangement. But so far I have no grip on the characters, other than their gender. I am undecided as to how much any of these characters will actually resemble me or Robert or James. In the meantime, Branwell and I have started writing a few paragraphs describing the location of the story, though I think he has no intention of seeing this through as he is working on his own novel. But I find his suggestions very helpful. We both have decided to set our tales in isolated moorland houses. In my story one of the first lovers lives there, a misanthrope who has cut himself off from human contact, still grieving for his lost love. I feel the stirrings of something important in this work. D.v. I can make a good job of it.[*]

EJB

Having read this entry several times, and also skipped ahead to find out how she developed her story, I am frustrated to find many of the questions I had at the time when she was writing it (and afterward) are still unanswered. But more of this later. At least from this entry I have learned exactly what part Branwell played at the beginning, and that for a time they worked well together. But I'm glad that he will never know that Emily later told me she based her Mr. Lockwood to some extent on his typically over-educated (and over-heated) language. In spite of his foolishness, and his melodramatic picture of himself, Branwell did genuinely suffer. His trials and troubles were nearly always of his own making, but he had a good heart underneath it all, and each of us loved him in our different ways. I have no doubt that God has forgiven the straying sinner, and welcomed him into his Kingdom.

AB

God may have forgiven him, but in my heart I can only feel regret for his wasted life and deluded conduct — and I am still very far from forgiving him as I remember all the pain he inflicted on us. My cruelty toward him in those last years was, no doubt, prompted in part by my own misery (of which he was completely unaware), but the hell he created for Papa was beyond anything I have ever witnessed.

As for Emily's reluctance to show her work to outsiders, to which she refers at the beginning of this entry, that was all part of the strange reclusiveness she exhibited ever since the death of young Robert Clayton — she became increasingly loath to interact with her peers. She was always a law unto herself, refusing to accept the opinions of others. After Brussels she mellowed somewhat, but she never accepted fools. Her comments on all those curates who were about the place at that time, and who were forever blathering on, airing their superficial and trivial opinions on all manner of subjects, were scathing. I will never forget the day she came into the dining room and saw three of them seated at the table, devouring Tabby's cakes and swilling tea — she gave them one fierce look, and after retrieving the article for which she had come, turned on her heel and escaped to the kitchen where I heard her say loudly to Tabby, 'How long do the pigs intend to stay at the trough?' I blushed at the time, but I savour that moment in my heart!

CB

I am feeling particularly cheerful this morning, quite bursting with feelings of good will to all men. I can only account for this unaccustomed state by some strange internal change in myself as nothing much has happened here — Papa is still exhausted by Parish problems, his eyes are growing steadily worse, and Charlotte is still depressed as she has had no word from M. Heger. Nevertheless, I have, over the last three months, written some verse of which I am very proud. And I am making great mental progress on the novel. But this is such a beautiful morning, Mother Nature beckons me to take up my shawl and walk, so I will stop now and give the dogs a good run. Today I plan to love everyone!

EJB

How I savour the joyousness of this entry! There are few, if any, like it in the entire Journal, and is it a salutary reminder that Emily at her best could spread more genuine good will about her than anyone I have ever known.

AB

I whole-heartedly agree! I know she undoubtedly appeared to the world as coldly reserved and reclusive, but when she occasionally lit up our lives with the dazzling brightness of her smiles and laughter, we all felt our spirits lift and soar. Even Papa would respond to her mood with light-hearted teasing, and Tabby would wax quite jovial and join in the fun to the best of her ability. Martha B., who adored Emily, would become quite animated, and we would hear her singing quietly to herself as she went about her duties. She has a sweet voice.

This entry, almost more than any of the others, makes me realize how great is our loss.

CB

Anne and Branwell have come home, but B only stayed a week and went back to Thorp Green. I wonder why? Anne, however, defiantly announced that she is not going to return. But there seems a great worry on her mind which she will not tell me about. I hope she has not left the Robinsons in bad temper.

We decided it would be a good time to take our first trip together, now that we have our own funds. We dithered and dallied trying to decide where to go. Finally Anne persuaded me that I must see York Minster, so off we went. On the whole I enjoyed the trip greatly, mostly because we played our new games all the way there and back. However, we had a few disagreeable hours in Bradford while the coach from Leeds to Keighley was being repaired (it had broken a wheel) — we were accosted by two young men, very much the worse for drink, who, seeing that we were unaccompanied, made lewd suggestions and one of them actually tried to embrace Anne! I quickly put him in his place with a smart slap, telling him to be about his business. The coach finally was ready for the road about 8 o'clock, so by the time we got to Keighley it was too late to reach home before dark, and we spent the night at the Fleece, and walked home in the morning. All in all, it was a real adventure!

I have made only a little progress in writing my story, but feel quite satisfied nonetheless, as I have formed a much clearer picture of the characters, and of the plot. Also, I have written several rather fine poems — not unconnected with the story. And, I must confess, not unconnected with Robert.*

---

* The poems Emily refers to are: 'Cold in the earth, and the deep snow piled above thee!' (March, 1845), 'Death that struck when I was most confiding...' (April, 1845), and 'Heavy hangs the raindrop...' (May, 1845). The last of these is accompanied by the initials 'A.E. and R.C.' And I have no doubt that 'A.E.' refers to Alexander Elbë while 'R.C.' is Robert Clayton. The first two contain some of Emily's finest lines, though the second is somewhat obscure in meaning as it is couched in an extended metaphor. We included both of them in our little book of poems but, as only two copies were sold, I transcribe one here in its entirety:

Death, that struck when I was most confiding,
In my certain Faith of Joy to be,
Strike again, Time's withered branch of dividing

My first triangle will consist of a spirited girl; a rough, ill-bred lad; and a young 'gentle-man'. She will be faced with the dilemma, just as I was, as to which she will choose. But

---

From the fresh root of Eternity!

Leaves, upon Time's branch were growing brightly,
Full of sap and full of silver dew;
Birds, beneath its shelter, gathered nightly;
Daily, round its flowers, the wild bee flew.

Sorrow passed and plucked the golden blossom,
Guilt stripped off the foliage in its pride;
But, within its parent's kindly bosom,
Flowed forever life's restoring tide.

Little mourned I for the parted Gladness,
For the vacant nest and silent song;
Hope was there and laughed me out of sadness,
Whispering, "Winter will not linger long,"

And behold, with tenfold increase blessing
Spring adorned the beauty-burdened spray;
Wind and rain and fervent heat caressing
Lavished glory on its second May.

High it rose; no winged grief could sweep it;
Sin was scared to distance with its shine:
Love and its own life had power to keep it
From all wrong, from every blight but thine!

Cruel death! The young leaves droop and languish
Evening's gentle air may still restore –
No: the morning sunshine mocks my anguish –
Time for me must never blossom more!

Strike it down, that other boughs may flourish
Where that perished sapling used to be;
Thus, at least, its mouldering corpse will nourish
That from which it sprung – Eternity.

I have read this poem over and over, and can only conclude that it must refer to the two deaths of the Clayton brothers; first that of John Clayton – 'Sorrow passed and plucked the golden blossom...', and then of Robert's – 'Cruel death!' Certainly John's death affected Emily far less that Robert's – 'Little mourned I...' And what a beautiful evocation of her love for Robert is contained in the lines 'High it rose, no winged grief could sweep it. Sin was scared to distance with its shine...'   Ed.

140

the lad goes away (why? I don't know yet) and she marries the gentleman. Then the lad returns after several years, now rich and educated, and she is torn between her new life as a respectable married lady, and her old loyalty and deep love for the other. Somehow, this kills her. But, now is begun a new cycle. On her death bed she gives birth to a child, a girl, who will be apex number one of the second triangle. In the meantime, the lad (now a man) has married, not for love but for revenge, the sister of the gentleman, and produced a male child; this boy is to be apex number two, and will marry the second heroine. The third apex is this girl's other cousin, son of her mother's brother, another rough lad analogous to the first one. Why he is a rough neglected boy I haven't worked out yet, but he must be the heir to his father's estate, so that when they all grow up, he can marry the second girl, uniting the two families, and live happily ever after. And I'm not sure how to dispose of the son of my first hero (and husband of my second heroine). He may be sickly and simply die of an illness. But the character who will carry through both parts of the story will be the surviving lover of the first girl, father of the weak boy who marries the second heroine. His great aim will be to revenge himself on the family of his dead love's husband (father of the second heroine). But he will be haunted by the dead woman's ghost. He must be a very strong character, as all the action of the book is initiated by him. Now it is time to find names for everyone, and work out how all this comes about.

Anne and Charlotte and I discuss names all the time; Charlotte is very clever at finding names which suit her characters, yet are not too far-fetched nor too obvious. Charlotte's hero is William <u>Crimsworth,</u> a Yorkshire name (Crimsworth Dene), but one which suggests both the good and bad elements of his character —Worth and Crime. Anne has picked 'Agnes Grey' for her heroine and we all like it — it is docile and self-effacing, with a suggestion of her strong Christian faith, just like her character. I am hard pressed to find such good names for my group. The two family surnames were not so difficult; the first will be Earnshaw. This is a common surname hereabouts, but it means 'eaglewood', and thus connects this old family to nature and to fierce pride. The other family (the 'gentlemen') will be called Linton (after a village north of here), a word suggesting commerce and civilization (linen-town). The problem is with the Christian names. I need names for the Earnshaws (brother and sister) and the Lintons (brother and sister), but mainly I must find distinctive names for the two boys who constitute my third apices.

EJB

How typical of Emily to start her novel with the geometry — the Eternal Triangle — and then to develop it into a complete family tree of perfect symmetry. I was always impressed by the way she began with a complete, almost architectural, outline of her story, even before she had the characters fully in mind. I certainly felt that Agnes Grey and Helen Huntingdon were very minor specimens next to Catherine Earnshaw, even though I will always consider WH to be a monstrous creation. Yet it was so solidly constructed, so rich in its depiction of relationships, whether for good or ill, I think it will stand to the end of time as a strange and fascinating edifice for all who attempt to storm its walls. And the beauty of the language surpasses anything I have read in the novels of earlier times. Even Charlotte, for all her great talents and expanded world-view, cannot touch Emily for economy of expression and lyrical precision. But, of course, it is a book without any redeeming moral quality, and as for what its message is — well, I remember Emily used to say, 'We are as God made us, and so be it.' This is a message I find impossible to accept. Surely God made us with the ability to improve morally, and with His help, to attain a place in His Heavenly Kingdom. There seems to be no place for free-will in Emily's view of humanity. And yet she herself behaved as if there were.

AB

I had not re-read Wuthering Heights since it was written, when we three all read and commented on each other's work. Even then I found it a frightening book (Emily thought I was either mad or silly) but I was not unaware of its power, nor of the supreme intelligence evinced in its construction and expression. There are many little inconsistencies in it, I believe, mainly due to the need to expand it, but they are minor, and had she lived, I think Emily would have amended the second edition herself. If only she had lived…

As for its message, it seems perfectly clear to me that the book has no message, and was not intended to have one. Emily once said she disliked novels with 'messages', and she would never degrade the reader by presuming to lecture him. I believe that perhaps she began to write WH in the hope that it would help her to understand what had happened to her all those years ago, but, as she says, the story took her beyond that goal, took on a life of its own which she was powerless to control. I am well aware, from my own experience with Jane, that this can and does happen.

I read with interest Anne's remarks about Emily's 'philosophy'; they brought back many a long argument we had at that time. And I tend to agree with Emily — we do seem to be born with deep and unchangeable traits, many of which are not admirable. Yet I cannot accept that the desire to become better is not also an inborn longing, and that the need to strive to better oneself is a necessary component of the desire for self-respect — a desire which, I think, is a basic element in all men.

CB

Dr. Scoresby was with us for tea last Sunday — and we had entertained Mr. Eggleston at dinner on the same day! It was the occasion of the yearly Sunday School celebrations, for which they both preached special sermons. It was a very busy time for us all, and it was a great pity that Charlotte was not yet home from her trip to Hathersage — Anne and I, with Martha's help, had to undertake all the cleaning and cooking by ourselves. Tabby sat in her chair and offered occasional comments and words of warning (Watch them pataties don't burn! —look to fire — it's gooin aht! etc), but we managed very well.

Mary Taylor has gone to New Zealand. She sailed last March, and we have had two letters from her en route. How I envy her!

EJB

My uneasiness over Branwell and Anne's return home has now been explained. Branwell has been summarily dismissed, apparently for his liaison with Mrs. Robinson. He is very distressed — not because of his dismissal — but only because he is prevented from communicating with the lady. Charlotte is furious with him, and can hardly bear to speak to him, and Anne appears to have completely given up trying to help him. I pity him greatly, but I do wish he would pull himself together. That relationship has no future, and he must force himself to understand this. I am trying to encourage him to continue with his novel, or at least to help me, but he is now so distracted that it is very hard to persuade him to get down to any real concentrated effort. So I have before me two excellent examples of the different ways one can behave when falling in love with a married person: Charlotte has driven herself inward, though she still writes to M. Heger. She, at least, has disciplined herself never to hope for more than the occasional kind word. Branwell, on the other hand, seems to expect a great deal more, even that Mrs. R might leave her husband, or at the very least, that she would meet him in secret. Poor fool. John Brown escorted him to Liverpool at the end of July, in the hope that a new scene would rouse him from his apathetic melancholy. It seemed to work, at least for a time.

Meanwhile, I am hard at work on several projects. I have nearly finished writing the Life of the Emperor Julius and the novel is making progress. I have finally, I think, decided on the Christian names for my characters. The names are so important, it is impossible to think of them as people until they are named. The two 'heroines' will both be called Catherine (daughter named after mother, as was true in our family). I love the name Catherine (I took this directly from Sir Walter — Catherine Seyton in The Abbot). The rest will have names that suggest something of their character, or their function. Catherine's unpleasant brother is to be Hindle, or perhaps Hindley, another common surname in these parts, but mainly because it is an animal name, 'hind', and also because 'hind' means a farm servant, very low. It would have been more accurate to use 'Hartley', hart being the male deer, but its second meaning 'heart' is not appropriate. The 'gentleman' will be Edgar, definitely not a local name, and was inspired by Edgar in King Lear. Also, it is not a beautiful name, as I don't want him to excite too much sympathy. His sister will be Isabella, which is a beautiful name but which I hope will suggest a certain frivolousness. Am still at a loss for a name for my first hero, but I think I have found a good name for the hero of the second triangle – Hareton. Branwell had a good friend named Ayrton when he was in Broughton, so the name does not sound so very unusual. But mainly I was thinking of the Heatons of Ponden, — that house is constantly at the back of my mind when I picture the early interior scenes at the home of the Earnshaws. But by putting in the R (secretly, for my Robert) and reversing the two vowels, I achieve a good animal (hare) and then the 'ton' (or town) suggests the union of nature with civilization, which is his function in the story — the uniting of the Earnshaws (nature) and the Lintons (civilization), in his marriage to the younger Catherine.

I forgot to mention, another new curate arrived in May, a Mr. Nicholls. He seems a competent and sober man, very tall and commanding in appearance. The fact that he is an Irishman pleases Papa, as well as his 'sound' theology.

EJB

The 'naming' of our characters was good fun, rather like playing a game. I am sorry Emily didn't mention one name, however — Frances, the young wife of Hindley Earnshaw, and also the name of the heroine of Charlotte's 'Professor', Frances Henri. I have long puzzled over why they both picked that particular name; was it coincidence? Or is there some significant meaning in it?

We three were working closely together at that time, reading and discussing our work, arguing and planning. Yes, a happy time. Sadly it didn't last. In those days I thought that Wuthering Heights would achieve for Emily a final resolution of her agonizing conflict over Robert C. and James G., and that the union of Hareton (a perfect representation of Robert!) and the younger Catherine would somehow satisfy her. Of course, I was wrong; she could never forget that Robert had died, and she always felt that she was in some way responsible. Though she never told me so, I know that the passage which most moved her was the elder Catherine's harrowing death scene in which she tells Heathcliff 'If I have done wrong, I'm dying for it. It is enough!' Emily often wished for her own death — we had no presentiment in the those days that her fatal day was so near at hand.

AB

Anne and I are finally starting to discuss our first novels. And I have admitted to her that The Professor was as painful to write as it is to read. I still hope to revise it and someday see it in print, but at the present time, it revives so may unhappy memories, that it must simply stay in the cupboard. Anne's Agnes is not unlike my William Crimsworth in some ways. Both suffer greatly under the burden of teaching the young, but Agnes triumphs in her quiet way, while William is a sad specimen of self-delusion and, though he finally marries Frances, it is she who triumphs. I hated myself so much when writing it, I was unable see him as an independent character. Frances, on the other hand, has much of Emily in her. How I miss her. She always hated The Professor, and she was right; it was an ill-advised, premature undertaking.

148

As for the name Frances, as I told Anne this morning, it really was a coincidence. Emily chose it because it is rather uncommon in Yorkshire, and for no other special reason. I chose it because it has French overtones, and because it is so like a man's name (Francis). I wish now I had written The Professor in the third person; perhaps then I could have seen everything more clearly. On the other hand, I probably could not have written it at all. Well, my current book is all in the third person, and I think it will be the better for it, if only I can finish it.

CB

At last, I have a name for my hero. He will have only one name as he is an outcast, and no one knows his real name. Haven't yet worked out how he becomes a ward of the Earnshaws — is he a natural son of Mr. Earnshaw and brought home on the death of the mother? Or is he a runaway, found by the old man and brought into the family? Or should I make his appearance on the scene ambiguous? In any case, his name is to be Heathcliff — 'heath' for our moors, and it goes well with the stern and dramatic word 'cliff'. It came to me one afternoon when I had walked up to the secret quarry with Keeper. As I entered it from below, I saw before me the high stone cliff, crowned with heather, and the word 'heath-cliff' leapt into my brain fully formed. It suggests something even more fundamental than my animal names — the primal world of nature, abiding and eternal. Also, Scott uses the name Earncliff, and I like the underlying suggestion of a connection with the Earnshaws. I daresay no reader will notice this, but I find it satisfying.

Of course, the son of Heathcliff and Isabella will be Linton Heathcliff — he will unite the worst characteristics of his parents, the weakness of his mother's family, and the selfishness of his father.

Now to name the houses of these families. The Lintons will live in an elegant newish house. In my mind's eye I see it as looking a bit like Woodlands, but perhaps located closer to the river like Springhead. The connection of those two houses with Greenwood families was the starting point, of course, as my erstwhile suitor, James Greenwood (of Springhead), is my model for the young Edgar Linton. I see the Lintons' house located in the bottom of a valley, with gardens and a park, all very gentrified and soft. I shall call it something-Grange — perhaps 'Threshfield' or 'Thruscross'; both are villages near Linton, according to our map, and both have a suitably gentle sound.

The other house, that of the Earnshaws, will be much older and located high up on land taken in from the moors, subject to the full onslaught of the elements — wind, rain, snow, etc. I see it rather like the old house at Ponden on the outside, but located even further out, higher up, just on the edge of the great moor that stretches away into Lancashire, perhaps where the three Withins stand. As for its name, it will be something Heights. I'll ask Tabby. I need a local word to suggest wildness, and strong winds.

Enough of this. My brain is spinning.

I had a strange dream the other night, if it was a dream — I dreamt I was lying on my bed (as I was in fact), but in a strange room, very dark and cold. Perhaps my candle had just burnt out. Suddenly I felt a great weight upon me, and the sense of being shackled, unable to move. It was as if I were not only imprisoned, but also enchanted by some evil spell which left me petrified, my limbs devoid of all motive power. At first I was frightened, but slowly I began to have the strange sensation of floating, losing contact with my bed, and then the air about me began fill with a beautiful reddish glow, and I felt a great rush of inward feeling, so intensely pleasurable I thought I must be dying and my soul was being poured into the Universe. Then it faded and I woke up, only to find that my book had fallen on my chest, and I was again in my familiar little room. Yet it was a wondrous experience, one I will never forget.

EJB

How fascinating to read these entries. Emily very rarely mentioned Robert or James while we were constructing our stories, though we often spoke about names and places. I should have seen immediately that the location of Thrushcross Grange and Wuthering Heights reflected not only the nature of her characters, but was actually closely connected with the homes of James Greenwood and the Heatons of Ponden. Charlotte has suggested that perhaps Emily was also thinking of Upper Ponden as the location for Wuthering Heights; it is the last house on Crow Hill before Stanbury Moor becomes uninhabited, and there were Claytons (the family of Robert's uncle) living in that house for many years.

As for Emily's dream, I can only say how much I envy her.

AB

Emily wrote of this dream — it is contained in that extraordinary poem she caught me in the act of reading that fateful day when I trespassed on her papers.[*] That was the ill-omened start of our

---

[*] The poem referred to begins: 'Silent is the house – all are laid asleep...' It is dated 9 October 1845. A shortened version of this poem appears in out little book of poems, entitled 'The Prisoner, a Fragment.' The significant lines are:

He comes with the western winds, with evening's wandering airs,
With that clear dusk of heaven that brings the thickest stars.
Winds take a pensive tone, and stars a tender fire,
And visions rise, and change, that kill me with desire.

Desire for nothing known in my maturer years,
When Joy grew mad with awe at counting future tears.
When, if my spirit's sky was full of flashes warm,
I knew not whence they came, from sun or thunder storm.

But, first, a hush of peace – a soundless calm descends;
The struggle of distress, and fierce impatience ends.
Mute music soothes my breast, unuttered harmony,
That I could never dream, till Earth was lost to me.

Then dawns the Invisible; the Unseen its truth reveals;
My outward sense is gone, my inward essence feels:
Its wings are almost free – its home, its harbour found,
Measuring the gulf, it stoops, and dares the final bound.   Ed.

literary careers.

As to the identity of all her houses, I am gradually coming to fully realize why Emily was so opposed to revealing our identities. Had it been known that the author of Wuthering Heights was Emily Brontë, there are several inhabitants of this neighbourhood who would immediately have guessed the origin of the story from the location of those houses, and therefore the identity of some of the characters. But her own identity must be revealed eventually — Emily's genius deserves to be recognized.

CB

As the result of my own untidiness I am embroiled in a sharp disagreement with Charlotte. How could I have been so careless! I had been working on a new poem, with all my papers spread out on the table, including the Gondal poems book. Anne was upstairs sewing, and Charlotte was helping Martha with the washing in the back kitchen. Papa called me into his study to read a letter to him which had just arrived, and I left the table with all its clutter, crossed the hall to the parlour, and completely forgot about my own work. Papa had a long letter from London regarding our new peal of bells (request for payment, arrangements for delivery, etc.). He and I became engrossed in the details of the matter. When I finally left him, over half-an-hour later, and went back into the dining room, Charlotte was standing by the table, with the Gondal poems book in her hand, reading quickly. I was dumb-struck. She turned suddenly, dropping the notebook. 'Oh, Emily, I... I didn't hear you come in...' 'Obviously', say I, very coolly. 'Well,' says she, 'I saw your papers on the table, and I was curious to see how your novel was progressing, but then I saw the poems...' 'So I see', I respond. 'Do I read your poetry without your permission? Do I even read your story? My God! How could you do such a thing!? These verses are private!!' I was trembling with rage, and advanced two paces. She fell back against the table, raising her arm to protect her face — I really think she thought I was about to strike her. 'Stop, Emily, please. I'm sorry... it's just that... I mean, this poem...' She shakily picked up the notebook, and turned to the last page I had written on. 'Do you have any idea how good parts of this are?' I was surprised by this new tack, and could think of no response. She took courage from this and dared to go on. 'But tell me about this one you wrote in May...' At that point I snatched the book from her — I knew which one she meant.* 'That poem', I whisper, 'does not concern you. Now, please leave my papers alone in the future.'

For two days now we have not spoken. Anne thinks I am being too harsh, but I truly feel violated.

EJB

---

* The poem referred to here is the one beginning, 'Heavy hangs the raindrop...' beside which Emily has included the initials, 'A.E. and R.C.', dated the 28 May, 1845. I have no doubt at all that A.E. is Alexander Elbë and R.C. is Robert Clayton. Ed.

That was a terrible time — the worst we had ever experienced among the three of us. Emily's fury was indescribable, like an equinoctial storm, or deluge. She gathered up all her papers, stuffed them into her desk box and, clutching it to her bosom, rushed out of the house, not even taking her shawl. She was away for hours. When she returned she was still white with anger and shut herself in her room with her box, slamming the door so violently I think she damaged the door-frame. Charlotte and I sat huddled together in the dining room, not knowing what to do, afraid that at any moment this avenging virago would issue forth and annihilate us. Papa wanted to know what on Earth was going on, and Tabby and Martha both looked too frightened to ask. We told Papa that Emily was angry over a mess Flossy had made in her room, and had taken her out on the moor to punish her, and was now cleaning it up. Charlotte and I decided it would be advisable for me to sleep in Aunt's old room (now Charlotte's room) for a few days. The next day Emily came down to breakfast but refused to speak, and later went out again, even though it was raining. I have never seen anything like it. On the third day she appeared again at breakfast, and seemed a little calmer. After she went back to her little room, I ventured to go up and knock on her door. She let me in eventually, and we sat talking for over an hour. Of course I understood perfectly well why she was so angry. But I tried to concentrate her mind on our old ambitions to publish, and to assure her that if we took noms de plume, no one need ever discover her identity. But it was to be another fortnight before we could persuade her that the project was feasible. And her relations with Charlotte never quite regained their old friendly candour and camaraderie.

AB

As Anne says, it was like being hit by a whirlwind! Emily's temper, when fully unleashed, was a force of nature. But I stuck by my guns, and with the help of Anne we finally succeeded in dragging her reluctantly to the point of grudging acquiescence. I will always be proud of our achievement — Emily was a great poet, and the world will be richer for knowing her work.

CB

Over the last 10 days Charlotte and Anne have tried to wear me down. Charlotte is convinced that my verses merit publication, and she wants us to approach a publisher with a view to bringing out a little book of our best poems. Anne is very keen, as she has just written a poem of which she is very proud — it is called Vanitas. Charlotte is very dismissive of her own work, but says she could dredge up a few that are not too dreadful, and she continues to insist that my rhymes (I finally allowed her to read most of them) would be the jewel in the crown, and that they would justify publication on their own. All very flattering. But do I really want the great reading public to have access to my most personal thoughts and feelings? And what about all the Gondal references? No, I do not think this is a good idea.

In the meantime I am trying to work on my novel, though this dispute over the poems is very distracting. Nevertheless, I have hit on the best name for the Earnshaws' house. Tabby suggested it: Wuthering Heights. She says 'wuthering' means stormy and windy, so it is quite perfect. And it shall be the title of the novel, I think.

Charlotte, on the other hand, has hit a major snag, and has given up her novel for the moment. Small wonder she is so enthusiastic for the poetry. Anne, of course, has almost finished hers. It is charming, and very moving. I only wish her life might follow the same course. She, too, is eager to pursue the poetry project.

EJB

Well, I have given up the fight. I have agreed to allow Charlotte to go ahead with her plan, on the condition that we use pen names, and that I choose which of my verses are to be included. I will let them do all the work after that, except for the changes necessary to eliminate Gondal people and places. They can correct my spelling and punctuation to their hearts' content, and do all the fair copying — and find a mad publisher who is willing to humour them. I have also insisted that our 'noms de plume' be somewhat masculine. Charlotte agrees that the verses will be more fairly received by the critics if they are thought to be by men. My real motivation, however, is to more thoroughly conceal our identities.

The plan of the novel is going along very quickly now. I want to present the actual story through the eyes of the housekeeper who has witnessed all the main events, but doesn't necessarily know everything, and may not fully understand what she does report. To intensify this effect, I shall introduce the book through the eyes of an outsider (a southerner, of course) who manages to misunderstand everything. He speaks the way Branwell used to do, very pretentious. This will be rather comic, but it also will give the reader a sense of mystification, even dread. I want to achieve the effect of great depth, slowly realized, as if one were looking into a pool, and at first one sees only the surface reflection of one's own face, but slowly the reader will see the strange fish swimming in the pool, and finally he may see right down to the murky depths at the bottom. Well, my girl, you certainly have your work cut out.

I have written and rewritten the first three chapters (Branwell no longer helps — he is hopeless), all the while letting the later story develop in my mind. Now I must get down to the basic narration by Mrs. Dean (my housekeeper at Thrushcross Grange, formerly at Wuthering Heights, a kind of blend of Tabby and myself). I am still worried about how to introduce Heathcliff into the Earnshaw family. I originally thought he might look a bit like Dr. Scoresby, but ever since Mr. Frederick Douglass arrived for his grand abolitionist speaking tour of these islands, I have pictured Heathcliff as a half-caste, quite dark.* The suggestion that he comes from a darkly alien and mysterious background creates great opportunities for later conflict and drama; he will cause havoc in the settled and traditional world of the Earnshaws and the Lintons, both old, established families. Would it have been possible for Mr. Earnshaw to have fathered a child by a black woman? I do know tales of runaway slaves not far from here in Dent Dale and in Westmoreland — rumours abounded at Cowan Bridge when we were there, and several years ago Papa heard from Mr. Sedgwick of Dent terrifying reports of murdered black servants there.** And Charlotte also heard strange reports when she was working for the Sidgwicks (their brother-in-law was once deeply involved in the slave trade), that blacks were still being smuggled into England and sold even after

---

* Frederick Douglass is an American escaped mulatto slave and one of the most eloquent spokesmen for the abolition of slavery. He made an extended speaking tour of Great Britain (1845-47) which was widely reported in all the newspapers. He is well-known for his superb speaking voice and handsome appearance. Ed.

** Emily is referring to the Rev'd John Sedgwick, the Vicar of Dent, and a member of the Committee which oversaw the Clergy Daughters' School in its early days. Papa had met him through our dear friend, Mr. Theodore Dury, Vicar of Keighley, and also a former Trustee of the School. One of Mr. Sedgwick's parishioners was Miss Ann Sill who lived all alone until her death (in 1835) in a grand house near Dent, staffed, it was said, by dozens of black servants. It was whispered that they had been slaves on her late brothers' plantation on the island of Jamaica, and were brought secretly to England before Abolition, and, though kindly treated by Miss Sill, were yet treated as slaves. Indeed, I have even heard a story, which I cannot vouch for, that when Miss Sill died, these poor souls ran away from the mansion, so great was their fear of her overseer, a cruel and pitiless individual. A 'hunting party' was then organized by this vicious man, and, so the story goes, they tracked down the negroes, cornering them in a rocky cul-de-sac by the River Dee, and slaughtered them all without mercy. Ed.

160

the trade was abolished.[*] Thus Heathcliff and Catherine would be half-brother and sister and perhaps the parallel with Lord Byron and his beloved half-sister Augusta will occur to the literate reader. In any case I may disguise these origins under a kind of fairy tale which Mrs. Dean heard as a child, but does not understand. Yes, I think that might serve, though it will confound the reader. I must stop now, and get on with dinner.

EJB

---

[*] In fact, Emily is slightly mistaken here. My employer, Mrs. John Benson Sidgwick of Stonegappe (née Sarah Greenwood), is the sister of Frederick Greenwood of Norton Conyers. Frederick is married to Sarah Staniforth whose brother is the Rev'd Thomas Staniforth. They are the children of Samuel Staniforth of Liverpool, a major slave trader in his day. Thomas Staniforth was nephew (by marriage) and also a great friend of Col. John Bolton of Storrs Hall, Lake Windermere. Bolton, too, was a slave trader and West India merchant, and it is thought that even after the trade was abolished in 1807, he continued to smuggle slaves into England, hiding them in the vast cellars of Storrs Hall before selling them on. Last year Thomas Staniforth inherited Storrs Hall from his aunt, Elizabeth Littledate Bolton, the widow of John Bolton. But I am sure that this dreadful illegal commerce had completely ceased by that time.   Ed.

The quite shocking suggestion that Catherine and Heathcliff were brother and sister makes their love forbidden by both the Law and the Church. Yet Catherine apparently only sees that it would disgrace her to marry Heathcliff because they would be poor! I asked Emily at the time to explain the fact that, as the Earnshaws have even given Heathcliff the name of a deceased brother, wouldn't Catherine have realized that he might also be her brother? Emily replied that Mr. Earnshaw would take that secret with him to the grave, and even if Catherine had suspected the truth (and she was less likely to, given the lack of any resemblance between them) she might not have appreciated its scandalous significance. All this takes a large pinch of salt — are we, the readers, really being asked to believe that not only was Heathcliff black, but he was also Catherine's half-brother? Well, she was certainly right to leave all these possibilities shrouded in mystery! However, I must admit that the parallel with Lord Byron and his half-sister Augusta is very persuasive. There is indeed something rather Byronic about Heathcliff. Lady Byron suspected her husband of either madness or murder or both, and Isabella says of Heathcliff, 'Is Mr. Heathcliff a man? If so, is he mad? And if not, is he a devil?'

AB

Suspension of disbelief must be exercised in so many ways with Heathcliff's introduction into the Earnshaw family. I must admit that I have always found Emily's 'explanation' pretty unbelievable, but I understood that this is probably what was intended. I remember saying to her at the time that on one hand Mr. Earnshaw had a stable full of horses, so why would he have walked all the way to Liverpool and back? And could he have accomplished this Herculean task in a mere three days? And, on the other hand, if he hadn't gone to Liverpool, where did he go and why was he lying? Is the reader really expected to see through these layers of obfuscation? Emily just smiled and said, 'If he is very clever, he will come to the right conclusion, and if not, well, at least he will be intrigued by the mysterious contradictions in the story, and see Heathcliff as something strange and alien from the very beginning.' But I had no inkling that all the while she was thinking of Mr. Douglass, and intended to suggest to the reader that Heathcliff was a runaway slave! Yet, I have lately gone back to the book and now I think I see what she was trying to do, — she has tried to convey how the condition of servitude (i.e. slavery) corrupted Heathcliff and how the role of master corrupted Hindley.

Yet I am still puzzled over Heathcliff; Emily has portrayed him as an out-and-out villain, almost a monster, and yet somehow, she seemed to expect the reader to sympathize with him. Perhaps this is because there is a little bit of Emily in him — the portrayal of his great grief on the death of Catherine is deeply felt, and Emily knew grief at first hand. And I am struck also by Heathcliff's grudging regard for Hareton — this tells me that Emily's identification with Heathcliff made it impossible for him (her) to hate Hareton, who is so clearly a romantic portrayal of Robert Clayton.

CB

February, 1846

Vicar

A few days ago we had another visit from <u>Dr. Scoresby</u>. His plan was to introduce Papa (and Mr. Nicholls and Mr. Grant) and the Grammar School Trustees to a possible replacement for Mr. Grant (who now has his own fiefdom — the new parish of Oxenhope) as the new master of the Grammar School. The new fellow is one James Stuart Cranmer — superb name, redolent of great swathes of English history. They all had dinner at the Black Bull, and Charlotte was on hand as companion to the interesting Mrs. Cranmer. I had hoped to go along, but Papa said that, sadly, I was not invited. He knew how disappointed I would be, so he asked Dr. Scoresby to call at the Parsonage before his return to Bradford. Accordingly Dr. Scoresby and Mr. and Mrs. Cranmer took tea here in the afternoon. I don't trust Mr. Cranmer — there is something false about him, something secretive — but Mrs. Cranmer appears to be highly intelligent. She is also very beautiful, and both Papa and Dr. Scoresby are quite enchanted. I must admit to a twinge of jealousy. But Dr. S is looking rather ill now, and much older; his resignation as our Vicar is, I fear, imminent. Papa has been trying to persuade him to stay, but to no avail.

My book continues to grow. I have reached a critical point — the beginning of the second part, in which Catherine's daughter has reached the age of 13, and is about to discover the tenants of Wuthering Heights. The last scenes of the first part (Catherine's death, primarily) were cathartic. But more of that anon — I must get back to work.

April, 1846

I have been writing furiously for the past six months, and now have a more or less completed manuscript. Neither Anne nor Charlotte is very happy with the result, both complaining that it is too violent, too amoral, and too irreligious. However they both own that it is compelling and powerful, which is approval enough. Anne's book, Agnes Grey, is well-written and will benefit the attentive reader — its lessons are edifying and highly principled, rather like the author. I find it a bit didactic, but nevertheless, it deserves a wide readership. Charlotte's effort, on the other hand, is artificial and very dreary, and it shows none of her superb talent for description and story-telling. I hope she will try her hand at another book, and draw much more on her personal experiences.

I have found my own experiences fundamental to the creation of my story, but it is fascinating to discover that once the characters are formed in one's brain, they begin to take over. Both Catherine and Heathcliff now tower over me, demanding that I expand their psychic world beyond death. When Catherine is dying, she says things that extend her character far beyond anything I had originally envisaged. The words seemed to reach me from outside my own mind. She says to Ellen Dean, '...you are sorry for me—very soon that will be altered. I shall be sorry for you. I shall be incomparably beyond and above you all.' I was quite shaken by these words; they reached into the depth of my soul. I found I myself unable for a short time to continue writing. Strangely, I laid aside the novel, and turned again to poetry.

The force of the conviction that I, too, would find triumph in death, was overwhelming and I was able to write what I think is my best poem. *

---

* The poem Emily refers to here is the superb "No Coward Soul", written on 2 January, 1846

No coward soul is mine
No trembler in the world's storm-troubled sphere
I see Heaven's glories shine
And Faith shines equal arming me from Fear.

O God within my breast,
Almighty ever-present Deity,
Life, that in me hast rest
As I, Undying Life, have power in thee.

Vain are the thousand creeds

Several days later, I returned to Wuthering Heights, but with a new sense of its purpose. Now, after Catherine's death, Heathcliff insists on remaining the most prominent player, even the puppet master (and am I the puppet?) almost to the end. His grief over Catherine's death was overwhelming and I was forced to relive my own despair when Robert died. When I began this book, I thought I could be calm and objective, and keep my characters at a sensible remove from my own feelings. Vain attempt! I thought Heathcliff's opposition would be the means of bringing Cathy and Hareton together (a kind of irony), but this has turned out rather differently. Now, although this still happens, it happens only because he gives up the struggle to keep them apart, and the two are united not because he opposes them but because he has ceased to oppose them. And he continues to dominate the entire second part off the novel, right up to his death which is again a kind of triumph. And even then, after his death, I was compelled to suggest that he

---

That move men's hearts, unutterably vain,
Worthless as withered weeds
Or idlest froth amid the boundless main.

To waken doubt in one
Holding so fast by thy infinity,
So surely anchored on
The steadfast rock of Immortality.

With wide-embracing love
Thy spirit animates eternal years,
Pervades and broods above,
Changes, sustains, dissolves, creates and rears.

Though Earth and moon were gone
And suns and universes ceased to be
And Thou wert left alone
Every existence would exist in thee.

There is not room for Death
Nor atom that his might could render void
Since Thou art Being and Breath
And what thou art may never be destroyed.

Ed.

and Catherine are at last reunited. They simply would not let me end the book with their 'eternal rest' in their graves. Originally I intended the words — '…and [I] wondered how any one could ever imagine unquiet slumbers for the sleepers in that quiet earth' — to be spoken by Nellie (Mrs. Dean), but now they are the last words of the book, and are spoken by Mr. Lockwood (he who misunderstands everything!) and the <u>true</u> last words are said earlier by the innocent little shepherd boy — 'they's Heathcliff and a woman, yonder, under t'Nab, un' Aw darnut pass 'em'.

Meanwhile, the poems are about to be published. Charlotte has conducted all the negotiations — the poems were accepted by Aylott & Jones in January (though, of course, we must pay for their printing and binding), we read the proofs in March. It is due to be offered to the public in May. The only sad consequence of this small accomplishment is that Branwell has become even more depressed. He has completely given up any attempt to finish his novel, and thinks only of his lady love, writing poem after poem about her. He is also drinking far too much. Perhaps we should have included him in our publishing venture — but Charlotte was adamant, and in any case, he would have been humiliated to tag along with us. One bright spot — a poem of his has just been published in the Halifax Guardian. He is currently thinking of going abroad, and has advertised for a position as a travelling companion, a plan which we all support, both for his sake and our own.

Papa's eyes are growing steadily worse; now Mr. Nicholls writes his letters for him, and guides him to and from the church. He is very despondent and fears he may become completely blind, but he also fears the operation to remove the cataracts. Charlotte has consulted a surgeon in Gomersal, who advises waiting until the growths are hardened and easier to remove, but I think that time is rapidly approaching.

Charlotte and I have started to make fair copies of our tales (Anne's was completed months ago), and hope to persuade our publisher to produce them as a three-volume set. Charlotte has already written to them, and we await the answer.

Fortuna favet fortibus!

EJB

I can hardly say which is worse — to be 'damned with faint praise' or to be damned with devastating criticism. Agnes Grey may not be as powerful as Wuthering Heights, but it is a good deal healthier. As for Emily's intransigence with regard to my criticism of WH, well, I knew that nothing I could say would alter her course. 'How can I change these people?' she would say. 'They won't let me — this is their story, whether we like it or not.' An unanswerable argument. I was feeling very alone and sad at that time. Charlotte and Emily were always busy, writing, arguing. I hated both their books, while they looked on mine with expressions of condescending approval, as a parent might admire the handiwork of a child, simply surprised that the little one has actually accomplished something! And Branwell was changed beyond recognition — he had heard that Mr. Robinson was on his death bed and was in a fever of anticipation. You simply couldn't talk any sense to him. On top of all, the Poems were about to be published, and I for one was dreading the reviews. I think I was, at that time, beginning to regret that we had ever started this publishing lark.

AB

Anne, how can you say such things? Emily and I both loved Agnes Grey! And it was *I* who was fiercely criticized by you and Emily — you both detested The Professor. I will admit, however, that Emily and I did work more closely together on Jane Eyre, but that was because we had both attended the Clergy Daughters' School, so it was logical that we should compare our experiences. And, to be frank, she was the best critic of the three of us, and the most outspoken. I appreciate and miss her penetrating intelligence now as never before as I struggle to make some headway with 'Hollows Mill'.

And as for your allegation that you regretted the publication of our poems, I simply do not believe you. I remember with vivid clarity the day our six copies arrived — you were as excited as a child at Christmas as we unwrapped the parcel. I fear you are remembering only the reviewers' lukewarm appreciation of your work.

But I am no longer able to rise to the defence of the

169

Professor. You and Emily were quite right to call it dreary. Perhaps someday I will try to resurrect it, but at the moment I am in a life and death struggle with my new book. Since Emily's death I have been unable to write much — my energies are depleted, and all seems 'flat and unprofitable'. Only this Journal rouses any interest, and, painful as it often is, still it is a last link with her, whom I loved above all others.

                                                                CB

It has been a singularly eventful summer. Branwell, who had become a trial and burden to us all, we thought was at last beginning to come to terms with his 'lost love'. But then suddenly Mr. Robinson had the audacity to die! So Branwell's mood vaulted into the heavens — he was fully convinced that he would now be able to marry his inamorata. He was swiftly disabused of this possibility when a visit from the Robinson's coachman confirmed the rumour that he was persona non grata at Thorp Green, and that he might be shot if he returned. Also he was told that Mrs. R would be disinherited if she so much as spoke to him. I am not sure that I believe this, but Branwell does, and he is now so downhearted I think he may go mad. While Charlotte and I were in Manchester to arrange for Papa's eye operation, Anne said Branwell behaved very badly indeed — he is increasingly dependent on alcohol and laudanum and in that confused and somnolent state, he might endanger the whole house with his terrible habit of trying to read in bed by the light of his candle.

Her remark was prophetic. While Charlotte and Papa were in Manchester for the cataract removal itself, Branwell came home late one night, tipsy as usual, and apparently went up to bed with his book and candle. Anne and I had both retired and were asleep. Suddenly Anne started up in bed, 'Emily, do you smell smoke?' She ran to Branwell's room and I flew down the stairs to fetch the water bucket. When I returned, she was frantically trying to wake him. The bedclothes and curtains were ablaze, and Anne and Branwell were both in serious danger. Suddenly I was possessed with the strength of ten — I pushed Anne aside, picked up Branwell and threw him in the corner. Then I tore down the curtains, pulled off the bedclothes, and threw them all in the middle of the floor. My hands were somewhat burned as was my face. 'Quick,' I cried to Anne, 'empty the bucket on them!' This doused the flames, but the room was filled with smoke. We opened the window to clear it. By this time Branwell was finally awake but very confused. So we took him down to the kitchen (Tabby was up by this time) and she made us all a cup of coffee. Branwell felt very guilty (as he should) and begged us not to tell Papa, but I said I hardly saw how this was possible. The lingering odour of burnt cloth and the absence of bed curtains are all too evident. And so it turned out; not only did we have to confess to Papa what had happened, but Branwell is currently sleeping with Papa until his own bed can be resupplied with bedding and curtains. Whether either of them gets much rest I truly doubt!

Papa's eyes are slowly healing, and he can almost see again. It is a great blessing. We and Mr. Nicholls still must read to him, and write his letters, but he can now easily find his way about the house and even to the church unaided. However, he is usually accompanied by Mr. Nicholls, who has been a great support to him in this difficult time, and who has taken on all his duties for the last several months.

Our manuscripts are making some small progress. In August they were returned again, and we sent Charlotte's Professor on to her in Manchester; it had been rejected outright. Agnes Grey and Wuthering Heights have had a slightly better reception, but nothing definite. Thos Newby has tentatively agreed to publication (at our expense) if Wuthering Heights, which is already too long for one volume, could be expanded to fill two volumes. So I am back at work, cudgelling my brain as how to augment it. Although Anne is not happy with my work, and implores me to soften some of the scenes (she says they are not realistic, which is not true), she is very eager for the books to be published, so I am doing my best. In the meantime both she and Charlotte have begun new books; both are ambitious works and will extend to three volumes. Charlotte has already written brilliantly about our time at Cowan Bridge, and has a good plan for the love story, very dramatic, and I think it will be successful. Her heroine, who is to be a small, plain orphan (Charlotte scorns our beautiful heroines), is somewhat based on herself, and so far it is very compelling. She lately received another letter from our old school friend, Mellaney Hayne (now Mrs. Storrs, recently married to a clergyman,

172

and living in Nova Scotia), and it seems to have revived very vivid memories.

Speaking of memories of Mellaney, Charlotte and I finally told Anne some of the fascinating (and shocking) stories about Lord Byron she told us when we were at Cowan Bridge — Mellaney's sister-in-law was his cousin.* He had just recently died when we were there, and everyone was talking about him, and the burning of his journal, and the scandalous and callous way he had treated his wife. Mellaney knew some very lurid details, particularly about the relationship between Byron, his half-sister Augusta (also a cousin of Mrs. Hayne), and Lady Byron. I think I may use a version of one of these stories in WH — Byron treated his wife appallingly, and I think Heathcliff will do the same to Isabella Linton.

Anne is being very secretive about her next book; she has made good progress with it but refuses to let me see it until it is completed. I suspect she fears I will either hate it or take offence for some reason.

Our little book of poetry has completely failed to find a market. We are not surprised, and we are not downhearted. Several of the reviews were favourable, which has given Charlotte great encouragement, and she is also crowing her vindication: 'Yours (i.e. mine) are recognized as the best of the lot!' She doesn't add, 'I told you so', but there is no need.

EJB

---

* To call Mellaney's sister-in-law (Emma Eardley Wilmot, who married William Burges Hayne in 1823) a cousin of Bryon and Augusta Leigh is not strictly accurate, but they were related. Emma's grandfather, John Eardley Wilmot, was the brother of Robert Wilmot, who married Juliana Byron, the sister of John Byron, who is the father of Augusta (Byron) Leigh and George Gordon, Lord Byron.   Ed.

It is highly instructive to read Emily's version of Branwell's downfall and his destructive night-time habits. I cannot but think she never took seriously the nightmare world he inhabited. She writes as if he were some sort of jest, and that his behaviour was simply another of his foolish idiosyncrasies. She was always inclined to see his bad or weak behaviour as a lack of will-power, something which could be overcome if only he would make the effort. She never understood that many people truly need help from a higher power, and that Branwell's tragedy was his weak faith in God. If only he had found it in his heart to lean on the Almighty... But he was caught in a downward spiral, and God seemed to be ever farther away. I pitied him greatly, but I was never able to help him.

AB

I wonder if Branwell really was mad. Papa still says he thinks that in the end Branwell was quite insane and beyond any help except that of the Almighty. Yet I know that I treated him very badly and will for ever feel the sharp pangs of conscience when I think of him — and Anne's comments have only intensified these feelings. I saw his predicament as a failure both in self-regulation and in moral character, and I blamed him for it. It is very hard to distinguish between intemperance and insanity when one appears to have led to the other.

But I have told Anne that she has sorely misjudged Emily in this. I know that Emily was profoundly saddened by Branwell's decline, but she had long since forgiven him his weaknesses. She told me many times that I should not blame him for that over which he had no control, but that if only I would make the effort to help him, he might regain some shred of his lost self-respect. But, alas, this was impossible for me. My own shaken confidence paralysed the ability I might once have had to rouse him from his stupor. Emily was the only one of us all who tried to pull him back from the brink of total despair. Her patience with him in that last year was astounding, and had it not been for his increasingly crazed dependence on laudanum and alcohol, she might have succeeded. But finally even she had to give up the fight.

CB

My problems with expanding Wuthering Heights were legion. I found I was unable (and unwilling) to add more to the basic story, so I decided to add verbiage around the edges by giving more space to Mr. Lockwood (that pompous popinjay) which lightens the tone (as requested), and to Nellie Dean. The latter character is dear to my heart; she may be conventional and not always sympathetic, but she is a worthy soul and I love her. I have also tried to pay closer attention to the precise dating of events in the story. Without this, some of the action may seem implausible, and the plot unnecessarily confusing. I expanded Isabella's letter to Nellie, which is now much too long, but a pleasure to write — the contrast between Joseph and Isabella is both highly amusing and pertinent. And it is useful to have another point of view regarding Heathcliff. But my greatest pleasure was in adding a few more details to a scene between young Cathy and Hareton. Their joy in each other brought back my love for Robert so intensely that I often found tears falling on my paper. The scene in which Lockwood overhears Cathy teaching Hareton to read, well, there is my portrait of Robert and all I wanted for us. Those few years of freedom and happiness are forever enshrined in my heart, surrounded by the luminous glow of childhood.

Another addition has been a better explication of the legal situation of the Linton estate and how Heathcliff got his hands on it. I borrowed several old books from Mr. Metcalfe, our solicitor, on the subject of inheritance law before 1833 — it is pretty confusing, but I think I understand what could have happened. And I have slightly expanded Cathy's diary entries in chapter 3. This was needed as it leads up to the incident in Chapter 6 in which Heathcliff and Catherine first go to Thrushcross Grange – I want to give the reader more than a fleeting glimpse of Catherine's true character as early as possible, so that the reader would be bemused and intrigued by her ghostly appearance at the window in Mr. Lockwood's 'dream'. I have a great sense of kinship with Catherine confiding her frustration, anger, and misery to the margins of an old book.

I am not sure that the first scene at the Grange is exactly as I want it, however. Perhaps it is still too close to what actually occurred when Robert and I trespassed at Woodlands, and were pursued by those vicious hounds. But on the other hand, it is such a perfect device to explain Catherine's discovery of the delights of genteel society — plausible and far more dramatic than my own experience. Yes, it must stand as it is — the entire subsequent arc of the story is initiated by this event.

EJB

I doubt that anyone reading WH would ever connect the scene at Thrushcross Grange with Emily's adventure with Robert at Woodlands. She discussed this with me at the time, and I assured her that the characters, Heathcliff in particular, were so well drawn, and so very different from the living models, that even if it became known that Ellis Bell was Emily Brontë, no one would suspect that the young Heathcliff was based in any way on Robert or that Catherine Earnshaw was a representation of herself. But Emily was never completely convinced of this, and was always concerned to hide her authorship.

My great difficulties with the book had nothing whatever to do with such concerns. Besides the story's complete lack of any moral standard, it was also the contradictory nature of Emily's philosophical outlook that caused me some disquiet. In spite of her insistence that man is incapable of changing his true nature, surely the great leap forward made by Hareton toward the end shows that Emily really did believe that one could overcome great obstacles with the help of a loving companion. Of course, she never accepted that the love of God was required for self-improvement, but I am convinced that deep down under her rather cynical view of humanity, she still believed that we are all on an upward journey.

AB

No, Anne is quite wrong. We discussed what she has written above while at breakfast this morning. I think I have convinced her that Emily, with her impeccable logic and consistency, would have explained the change in Hareton in the following way: Hareton has not <u>basically</u> changed at all. His degrading treatment by Heathcliff may have masked his intrinsic decency and intelligence, but Cathy's love only stripped away his rough, crude, churlish outer shell, and revealed his true and noble nature. This is demonstrated not only by his rapid response to Cathy's ministrations, but also to his poignant grief over Heathcliff's death. Only a truly good soul could feel love for his persecutor.

We then went on to that most interesting topic, Emily herself. Both of us have puzzled (separately) for years over the

did it change?

dramatic change in her character which occurred at the time of Robert's death. She was transformed in a few short days from a happy, if confused, adolescent to a secretive, reclusive woman. Even after she had apparently recovered from her great grief, she remained reserved and, in the presence of outsiders, cold to the point of rudeness. I wonder what she would have said if I had simply confronted her with this fact, and asked her how this fit with her firmly held belief that all men are born with a certain underlying immutable nature. Anne's explanation is simply that she had lost her faith in God and Man. But I think there is a more complex answer. Perhaps Emily was correct in thinking that we are unable by our own efforts to change our basic character, but now one must consider the effect of external events which impinge upon our lives. Surely when we are faced with momentous changes or happenings in our lives, they affect us deeply, and change us for good or ill. I think of the many deaths in our family, and how all of us (except possibly for Anne) were changed. When Maria died, it was as though Mother had died again, only much worse, as we were so close to her and she was our idol, our little mother. And when Aunt Branwell died, Branwell was heart-broken, and I think his 'love' for Lydia Robinson (17 years his senior) may have partly been the result of his great need for the love of an older woman to take Aunt's place. He certainly had never before shown any interest in women of that age. As for myself, Emily's death has changed me for ever. I can now clearly see that life rarely ends with 'happily ever after'; its only certain ending is the grave.

CB

We are all terribly excited by the progress of Charlotte's second book! Her last attempt to find a publisher for the first (The Professor) ended in failure, but that very publisher (Smith, Elder) intimated they would be interested in a three-volume effort. So Charlotte made haste to finish Jane Eyre, sent it off to Mr. Smith in August, and has now already received the proofs, and it will be published in October. And she is being paid for it! Meanwhile, Mr. Newby, who has had our revisions and corrections (and our money) for many months, shows no sign of making progress toward the publication of Anne's and my tales.

EJB

I can still vividly recall now how excited I was over the sudden revival of hope brought about by Mr. Smith's and Mr. William's gentlemanly critique of The Professor, and their immediate acceptance of Jane Eyre. Emily and Anne tried to join in my happiness, and I think they were genuinely pleased for me, especially as they had both disliked The Professor, and had been strong supporters of Jane, whom Emily described as 'a fiery little dragonette'. Anne, however, hard as she tried to look happy for me, must have felt some resentment. After all, her Agnes Grey was, like Jane Eyre, the autobiography of a poor governess, and comparisons between the books would be inevitable. No wonder she completely changed tack with Tenant. A mistake, certainly!

CB

Well, what a to-do! Since last I wrote, and it seems only a few weeks ago, the novel-publishing venture has taken another astounding twist. Jane Eyre is the literary sensation of the country! Not only is it selling well, but it is being very widely reviewed, and the reviews are generally favourable. Newby, of course, is rushing through the publication of Agnes and Wuthering Heights in order to take advantage of the furore surrounding Jane. I am beginning to wonder if he thinks that Ellis and Acton Bell are one and the same as Currer Bell. We expect our free copies to arrive in the next few days. Charlotte is elated, but tries to conceal it in deference to our feelings. But the strangest part is that because neither Papa nor Branwell (when he makes an appearance) have any suspicion of our clandestine doings in the great world of publishing, the conversation at dinner is very unnatural, as we try to talk of anything other than what has consumed all our waking thoughts for the last month. Charlotte says that perhaps when all our books have been published, then she will tell Papa about the success of Jane. As for me, I would prefer that no one ever found out that I had written W.H., particularly Papa, and have asked Charlotte not to say anything to him about it. She has promised, but I know she is dying to tell everyone about Jane, so I hope she will limit the revelation to her own work.

EJB

That was a chaotic time of mixed emotions. Happy as I was at the success of Jane Eyre, I was painfully aware that Agnes Grey would never look interesting in comparison with her. And I have to admit to feelings of resentment against her for taking my original idea (the autobiography of a governess) and turning it into a burning romance, complete with Gothic touches and the foul odour of vice and scandal, even crime. Well, obviously the reading public wants more than a plain story, plainly told. Tenant was planned as a riposte to both Jane and Wuthering Heights, full of scandal and vice, but also full of sincere moral teaching.

AB

I read Anne's comments last night before I went up to bed, and we have had a long talk about them this morning. Unfortunately Anne is not very well, so I had to be as gentle as possible. Nevertheless, I told her I was shocked to learn that the nature of Tenant was partially a reaction to Jane Eyre. I had no idea that Anne harboured these feelings of resentment, that I had 'stolen' her idea (Agnes Grey, the governess) and degraded it. I tried to convince her that this was far from the truth, and that the origins of JE came almost entirely from my own experiences, first at Cowan Bridge, and then at Stone Gappe and Swarcliffe. But I fear that Anne and I are now somewhat estranged, and for this I am more sorry than I can say.

CB

At last the excitement has begun to die away. Our books have all been published and reviewed, and suddenly we (or rather Currer, Acton, and Ellis Bell) have briefly been the centre of attention. Indeed, Charlotte's Jane Eyre is still the belle of the ball; it seems the entire reading public of these isles has read her story, and is consumed with curiosity to winkle out the identity of her creator. The reviews of W.H. and Agnes G., however, have not been so favourable; Agnes has been all but ignored, and W. H. roundly reproved for coarseness; but some reviewers, in spite of themselves, appear to be impressed. Ho hum.

I feel very uneasy with the success of Jane, as it is inevitable that soon Charlotte will want to claim authorship, and this will expose both myself and Anne. But I have made her promise that while I live, she will not give me away. Although I concealed as best I could my personal story under layers of dramatic fiction, it is still there, and I know the Greenwoods at least might recognize it, and it would grievously wound James. I don't mind what they say about the older Heathcliff, but young Heathcliff and Hareton, in particular, bear such a resemblance to Robert that those who remember him, and what happened to him, would never forgive me. It is sad enough to know that there may still be a few people who blame me for his death, but there are many more who, if they knew I had written about him – exploited his memory for financial reward... I simply couldn't bear it.

The strange aftermath of this period of hard work and then intense public attention is that I find myself unable to write even a line of decent verse. And the 'new' Gondal stories have paled into poor shadows. Wuthering Heights has ruined all that for me. And to cap it all, we have succumbed to colds and influenza.

EJB

The reception of Agnes was discouraging, but I refused to be downhearted. Tenant was nearly finished, and would, I was confident, not be ignored when it was published. At least AG was not condemned for coarseness and immorality. Emily's reaction to the reviews of WH was predictable — she feigned complete indifference. But I could see from her stony face that she was not happy. The ordeal of being judged was something she had long avoided and no matter how ignorant and narrow-minded were her critics, this was a new and devastating experience for her, and she faltered before it. Small wonder she decided never to write another novel.

AB

Here at last is something Anne and I agree upon. Emily was deeply stung by the reviews of Wuthering Heights, and for all her apparent nonchalance, her entire attitude to writing anything completely changed. She spent these latter days playing the piano and reading, but I never saw her pick up her pen again to indite anything more serious than a letter or her accounts. No, that is not completely true — there was one later poem. This last poem is so dreary, so filled with despair, I turn cold at the very thought of it.*

CB

---

* Emily's last poem is dated 13 May, 1848, and reads:

Why ask to know what date, what clime?
There dwelt our own humanity,
Power-worshippers from earliest time,
Feet-kissers of triumphant crime
Crushers of helpless misery,
Crushing down Justice, honouring Wrong:
If that be feeble, this be strong.
Shedders of blood, shedders of tears:
Self-cursers avid of distress;
Yet mocking heaven with senseless prayers
For mercy on the merciless.

It was the autumn of the year
When the grain grows yellow in the ear;
Day after day, from noon to noon,
The August sun blazed bright as June.
But we with unregarding eyes
Saw panting earth and glowing skies;
No hand the reaper's sickle held,
Nor bound the ripe sheaves in the field.

Our corn was garnered months before,
Threshed out and kneaded-up with gore;
Ground when the ears were milky sweet
With furious toil of hoofs and feet;
I, doubly cursed on foreign sod,
Fought neither for my home nor God.   Ed.

Anne has nearly finished her second novel, The Tenant of Wildfell Hall, and has at last permitted me to read it. Like Agnes G. it is very didactic, but much more dramatic. However, it is not in any way autobiographical, and to write from the point of view of a married woman (and an unhappy one, at that) with a child, is perhaps stretching the limits of her imagination too far. I find it unconvincing. She defends it vigorously, and says I did the same thing in W.H. (write about something I have not experienced) with what she calls my shocking and vicious account of Isabella Linton's marriage to Heathcliff, saying I never had such an experience myself. Well, I say, that is much easier to imagine than an entire life with a profligate husband, and what it is like actually to be a mother. In Wuthering Heights I was careful to avoid writing about the relationship between mother and child, as that is something I feel I am not only incapable of delineating, but also unworthy to attempt. There are many fathers in my story whose relationships to their children are described (for good or ill), but not one mother. Yet, in my heart, I know that Anne, who has always yearned for motherhood, might wish to bend her imagination in this direction, and I am sorry that I was so sharp with her.

But there is now a coldness between us, which I regret but cannot change. I am sorry she has written Tenant, which is clearly a response to Wuthering Heights. Anne and I are so different in how we see the world — she thinks it is possible to improve mankind, and suggests small steps, guided by Christian principles, in that direction. Whereas I see mankind as irredeemably and deeply flawed in ways that cannot be altered. Selfishness, greed, self-delusion — these are things which no amount of Christian exhortation and charitable works will ever change. The giver of charity may benefit from a sense of his own worthiness, but the recipients are either humiliated and debased, or resentful and ungrateful. I know this from my misguided attempts to help our own poor. If it were possible somehow to arrange the world so that man's faults and follies might work to the benefit of the general populace, we might expect some improvement in the condition of all, but I see no way that this can be accomplished, except occasionally and by accident.

Charlotte and I often discuss this vexed problem; she defends Anne's point of view, but her heart is not in it. Can human nature be improved? I think she is as sceptical as I, but she refuses to acknowledge it. She says that one must believe that it is possible, and endeavour always to improve oneself, even if one is doubtful that mankind will ever rise above its present state of apathy and delusion. The upshot of all this is that Charlotte has already begun to outline her next novel. She feels she needs to write something connected with the present condition of England, which at this time is truly appalling. Conditions are even worse now than in 1842 and '43 — manufacturing hadn't fully recovered from that downturn before this one began, and now we have the added problem of thousands of starving Irish refugees flooding into Liverpool. So the labouring classes are on short-time or less, or their jobs are taken by Irishmen willing to work for half the pay.

I, too, have been thinking of writing a work on this subject; Mr. Newby is eager to publish it, though he has advised me to work slowly and carefully. Last week I walked over to Wilsden to talk to Mr. Butterfield — he knows a vast amount about the Chartists, the law, and commerce.* I asked him if he thought it would be suitable to set a story in 1842 against the background of the Plug Riots and the great march on Bradford. I suggested that I was inquiring for my brother who was looking for a subject for a novel. I apologized that Branwell was too ill to come and speak to him himself, and at that point Mr. Butterfield gave me a stern lecture on Temperance to take back to Branwell; he had obviously heard of his sorry state. But, pleased as he was

---

* Francis Butterfield of Wilsden, Methodist preacher, staunch Chartist, and Temperance advocate. He was also a friend of the late poet, John Nicholson, who was a friend of Branwell in his days at Bradford.   Ed.

to hear that Branwell (or 'Mr. Patrick', as he called him) was making the effort to write a novel, he said the choice of subject was very unfortunate as it would only inflame the existing climate, and would make more trouble for everyone.* This has put a serious damper on my intention, even my desire, to undertake a new work. Charlotte, however, is pushing on with hers and now intends to set her story back in the time of the Luddites, and to be as matter-of-fact and impartial as possible. I wonder if she has really understood the problems, or if she has enough sympathy and compassion to deal with this titanic subject.

So now I have no writing in hand — no more Gondal, nor poetry, nor new story. I am reduced to spending my time with housework, sewing, or reading, and playing the piano. If only spring were here, I could walk out, but the weather has been endless wind and rain. Mr. Newby writes that he is eager to publish my next novel, but I am so low at present, that he may have to wait a very long time indeed. My cold continues unabated. Oh, if only spring were here.

EJB

---

* In the spring of 1848, there was social unrest all over England, and on the 10th of April, Fergus O'Connor presented to Parliament the Chartist petition containing over 5 million signatures. Nothing came of it directly, but interest in the condition of the working classes is increasing. The admirable Mrs. Gaskell has written a fine novel on the subject (Mary Barton), which so moved me that I briefly considered abandoning my own efforts to complete *Shirley*.   Ed.

No matter what Emily and Charlotte opined, I am sure I was right, and I found their pessimism very sad indeed. Nothing I could say would persuade them to see my real reasons for believing that mankind was improvable. The great difference between myself and Emily was that she no longer accepted the love of Jesus, that she did not even believe in Him as the Son of God. And without the help of our Saviour, we have no hope of moral progress; how can we rise above sin and death without His help? As for Charlotte, at least she accepts that an individual can strive for perfection, but she thinks this can be achieved purely through one's own efforts, without help from the Almighty. But I know in my heart that this help is always present, and the true path, revealed by Him, which leads to Salvation, is perceived dimly even by the most vicious of souls. They lack only a clear understanding of the Way, and it is the duty of all true Christians to point this out, and encourage the weak and ignorant to see the great reward which will be theirs. And I believe most ardently that all of us, the sinners and the God-fearing alike, will reach the Heavenly Kingdom. He loves us all equally, and though the path to Glory may be longer for some, in Eternity we shall be together for ever.

AB

Anne's deep faith and trust in God is very moving. How can I say to her, as she faces the near certainty of her own early death, that I have doubts about the after-life? But the longer I live, the more I am convinced that what matters far more than the expectation of eternal life is the reality of our lives in this world. And what we do here should not be done with our eyes on our reward after death, but simply because it is good and right. As Emily so often pointed out, none of us has any assurance that such a thing as life everlasting exists, so it is pointless to base any actions here on Earth on that assumption.

Emily had her own ideas about what happens after death. I have now reread all her poems many times over, and some are contradictory and many are still incomprehensible to me. But the later ones all seem to point to a conviction that she would 'brave the darkness of the grave' on a path leading to 'Rewarding

Destiny'. She wrote this while she was in the early stages of WH, but before I had 'snooped' into her desk box. It is one of her greatest poems, and I insisted it go into our little book of verse. But she never explained to me who her 'Glad comforter' was.[*] At first I thought she meant some kind of angel, but now I begin to wonder if she was not actually beginning to believe that the soul (ghost?) of her early love, young Robert Clayton, was appearing to her. I think of that astounding scene in WH where Heathcliff sees the ghost of Catherine finally before his bodily eyes, shortly before his death. I have always felt that Emily was able to see things that were invisible to us. She was an extraordinary creature.

But to return to the everyday world of commerce and business to which she referred in the Journal: a stark example of the desperate condition of trade occurred very close to home in the summer of last year — Bridgehouse Mill, the largest mill in the village, was stopped, and Mr. James Greenwood of Woodlands faced bankruptcy. Hundreds of operatives are now reliant on the Poor Law Guardians. Papa has long since forgiven Mr. James for his political and religious antagonism, but he told me that it was his opinion that the Greenwoods have been brought down by their own hubris and extravagance. In the village many are saying that they (the Greenwoods) and the Sugdens are still cursed by the scandal of Mr. Sugden's seduction of his sister-in-law which continues to rumble on. This is pure superstition, of course, but I have heard tales that the spirits of his dead wife, poor Mary Ann Sugden, and her mother, Mrs. Greenwood, have been seen and heard wailing in the garden of Bridgehouse.

---

[*] The poem referred to begins, 'How beautiful the Earth is still...', written on 2 June, 1845. The final verse reads:

Glad comforter, Will I not brave
Unawed, the darkness of the grave –
Nay, smile to hear Death's billows rave,
Sustained, my guide, by thee?
The more unjust seems present fate
The more my spirit swells elate
Strong in thy strength, to anticipate
Rewarding Destiny!   Ed.

As for my next novel, it has slowed to a halt. Emily was right as usual; I cannot see how to present the problems of both the mill owners and the mill workers in a balanced way — I simply do not know enough. And in my present state of mind, I am drawn more and more to telling a different story, one which is a homage to the dead. The character of Shirley is already taking the shape of Emily, as she might have wished to be, and I may even include a brief eulogy for Martha Taylor. Best to be faithful to what I know, and give up the vain ambition that my book can in any way affect the course of civilization.

CB

July, 1848

The end is now clearly in sight; Charlotte and Anne have just returned from London and the meeting with Charlotte's publisher and with Mr. Newby; the upshot is that not only do they now know that Currer Bell is Charlotte Brontë and that Acton is Anne, but Mr. Smith and Mr. Williams also know there is another Brontë sister, Ellis Bell, author of that terrible book, Wuthering Heights. How long before the whole country knows? I wish they had never gone — surely this whole matter could have been dealt with by post. Is not the evidence of our separate and distinct signatures sufficient to prove that there are three Bells? 'We are three sisters', Charlotte told them. I am betrayed.

Yesterday, as is our custom when the weather is fine, Keeper, Flossy, and I went for our usual walk up past Penistone quarry and out on to the moor. I was in a foul mood, because of C's & A's treachery, and felt the need of a more extended excursion that afternoon, so we took the path leading to the Withins. But I was strangely drawn to tarry a while at Far Slack. It has been many years since the Clayton family have lived there, and it looks different now. How time has changed everything. So we went onward and came to the entrance to our secret quarry. Ah, at least it has hardly changed at all. I sat on the great flat rock for a long time, remembering our games. This was the very place where Robert and I had first declared our love for each other, and every stone and mossy patch is dear to me. Then the dogs and I climbed to the top of the quarry, and I looked back across the valley to Ponden House. I wondered if I should go down and call on the brothers (with both their parents dead, life must be very hard, and I have not called on them for almost a year) — but Keeper was impatient to go on, so on we went. But not to the Withins — instead we followed the path that leads round the head of the great valley and finally we came to Ponden Kirk, one of our most loved places. Once upon a time you could see almost all the way to Keighley from here, but the air in that direction is now always full of dusky smoke from the factory chimneys of Haworth and

193

Keighley, so the hills between are indistinct and faint. There was no wind that day, and the sun was veiled by a thin mist. It was very quiet. I sat there for a long time, my eyes closed, thinking of nothing, lost in a kind of trance. Then, gradually, I became aware of someone sitting beside me. I felt a hand gently rest on my shoulder — then a cheek softly brushed mine. I was not afraid — I knew it was Robert. At last, I opened my eyes and turned to see, but could see no one. Yet the feeling of the hand on my shoulder lasted for many minutes. I write this experience down because I believe it was real and has great meaning. Not only was I myself aware of this ghostly presence, but Keeper also exhibited signs of interest — he barked and pranced about, wagging his tail vigorously — and when it was over, he came over to me and nuzzled my cheek. But poor Flossy cowered, and put her tail between her legs.

EJB

I have been dreading this entry. On that fateful day in London, we knew as soon as Charlotte said it ('we are three sisters') that we would have to admit to Emily our mistake. And Emily had even warned us before we went up to town that Mr. Smith and Mr. Newby were sure to decode the name Ellis Bell as that of another Bell sibling. We had meant to say he was our brother, but somehow the truth popped out of Charlotte's mouth before she could stop it. I had not seen Emily so angry since the time Charlotte 'happened upon' her poems. The breach was to be permanent after that. There was nothing we could do to gain her forgiveness. And I think it hastened her death. She seemed to long for it, almost to embrace it.

AB

There is no doubt in my mind that the trip to London was a huge mistake, and was motivated entirely by my own desire for recognition. It had very little to do with clarifying our identities to our publishers, though that was the excuse used. Mr. Smith and Mr. Williams were, of course, delighted to meet us, and our physical presence did prove that the Tenant of Wildfell Hall was not written by the author of Jane Eyre or Wuthering Heights, and that Acton, Currer, and Ellis Bell were distinct and separate individuals. But worse was to come when we confronted Mr. Newby. Determined not to repeat our error in identifying Ellis as a third sister, we stuck to our story that he was a man, our brother. Then Newby insisted that Ellis must therefore have written all the books (being a man!) and had forced us, his sisters, to connive in concealing his identity. Well, this was really beyond the pale, and I said to him, 'Then how do you explain the fact that Jane Eyre was not published by yourself?' He made up some silly story that it was not submitted to him because of Ellis's extreme concern to conceal his identity. I merely smiled at that, and said that he might avail himself of the opportunity of consulting Smith, Elder on that point. Too late I noticed Anne's warning look intended to remind me that Mr. Smith now knew that Ellis was a woman. Later I learned from Mr. Williams that Mr. Newby had finally been convinced that Ellis was not the author of any book other than Wuthering

Heights; after that he dropped all communication with Ellis and Acton Bell. And Mr. Smith and Mr. Williams have kept their promise not to reveal the gender of Ellis Bell to a living soul.

But I hope and pray that Anne is wrong in thinking that these incidents hurried Emily's death. It is hard enough to know she felt alienated from us in those last months. But I suspect that it was not our actions which accelerated her rapid decline; her account of the meeting with Robert's ghost (if that is what it was) may have convinced her that he was waiting for her, and perhaps she simply made haste to reach him.

CB

<hr />

Branwell is dead. We laid him to rest under the church floor this morning. Charlotte is ill with remorse and sorrow, and Papa is saddened beyond words. Anne and I, though we seldom agree on anything these days, both feel he has been delivered from his own hell. Anne is confident that God will receive the sinner with love and forgiveness, while I only hope that, if there is some kind of life after death, it is at least better than the life he has left behind.

I still have my old persistent cough and cold, and feel emptied of all energy.

EJB

Inserted here was Branwell's funeral announcement, a card edged in black, which read:

In Memory
of
Patrick Branwell Bronte
who died
September 24th, 1848
aged thirty years

---

true?

Anne and I, for our separate reasons, have just made a great bonfire of all our papers, even the Gondal Chronicles. At Charlotte's insistence, I have kept only the poetry. I have also burned all my letters, except for a few from Charlotte which she has asked to keep, and a few from Anne which I inserted in this Journal. Yes, I have even burnt my one letter from Robert.

My health is stubbornly refusing to improve and I want my affairs in order, in the likely event that I succumb. I will hand this Journal to Anne before I die, with instructions to read it if she wishes, and then to burn it.

EJB

————————————————

Those were dark days indeed. Our sacrificial bonfire took on the aspect of a sacred rite, marking the final phase of our lives together. I was quite content to see the great quantities of Gondal prose go up in smoke, but I held back many of her letters to me; I could not burn them, no more can I burn this Journal. As for our hundreds of pictures, saved since childhood, at least I persuaded her not to destroy them all, and she allowed Charlotte to look after a small group of them. When I, too, am gone, Charlotte must decide their final dispensation. And, though I have impressed upon her the necessity of destroying this Journal, yet I have serious doubts that she will be able to do so. I know I cannot.

AB

As I read these few final entries in Emily's Journal, I am beset with agonizing doubts about the future. I know that Anne will soon follow her sister to the grave, and then I alone must decide how to dispose of all these precious documents and drawings. Papa implores me to keep everything; he was very hurt, even angry, when he discovered that Anne and Emily had already committed many of their pictures to the flames. At the present moment I know I am incapable of destroying any sheet of paper which Emily has touched. Her absence overwhelms me.

CB

November, 1848

This will be my last entry in this Journal. I am very weak now, and have difficulty in breathing — even holding my pen is tiring. I am calm, and have no fear of death. The only disturbance to my tranquillity is the constant reminder that my father and sisters continue to hope for my recovery — they pester me with suggestions for medical intervention. But I know there is only one outcome for this malady, and I wish it to be quickly accomplished.

Emily Jane Brontë

———————————————————

23 December 1848

Emily died on the afternoon of the 19th of December. She was conscious almost up to the last moment. Charlotte and I agree that it is a blessed relief to know that she is no longer in pain, and, selfishly, that we no longer must watch her valiant efforts to carry out her daily chores, denying to us the great satisfaction of helping her. She was obdurate. But when it was finally clear to all that she was preparing to leave us, she entrusted this, her Journal, to me, saying I could read it after her death, but I must then destroy it. Will I be able to do this?

It is impossible to express the poignancy of her funeral. Mr. Nicholls conducted the service and the interment with great simplicity and dignity. Papa and Keeper led the mourning procession behind the coffin, Charlotte and I followed, Tabby and Martha walking behind us. There were only a few others in the church for the burial service, but I noticed several of them weeping openly. Keeper kept up a low moaning throughout the proceedings. He is sitting outside her bedroom door even now, as I write. Her mortal remains were laid to rest in our family vault with the five other dear departed. I am so tired I feel I could sleep for ever.

Anne Brontë

---

25 January 1849

I have decided that it is unfair not to let Charlotte read Emily's Journal. She is in such despair over her death, I think it may help her to begin to understand many things about Emily which puzzled her during her life, and perhaps she may find some comfort and peace of mind in this; and I hope she will be consoled by the knowledge that Emily died willingly, with no regrets, and with no hopes for her own life on this earth. May God sustain us in our time of sorrow, and prepare us for His Glorious Kingdom.

A. Brontë

---

25 February 1849

I find I am compelled to fill up the empty final pages of Emily's Journal, almost as if she were sitting by my side, saying, 'Go on Anne, don't waste all this good paper!'

There is nothing of importance to say, of course, but a few minor matters deserve mention. Both Papa and Charlotte have, like myself, succumbed to severe colds and influenza. They are both better now, but my own health is not very robust, and I continue to have some pain in my side, and a slight fever. I have been a very good girl, and followed the Doctor's advice in all things. We even have a fine new respirator which greatly helps my breathing. It has been very cold, and we keep all the fires going in every room, regardless of cost.

I try with all my strength not to think about the probable outcome of my illness, and I pray I will yet be spared for a few more years. There is so much I could do if I only I might feel well again. I often think that if I can survive until the spring, then I will recover.

Charlotte finds that work on her new book is impossible; she sent the first volume up to London in September, but seems doubtful that she will be able to finish it. I am hoping that reading Emily's Journal may encourage her to go on. She has already decided that Shirley will be a pen portrait of Emily, and I think she feels she knows her better now that she has read the Journal. But at the moment she lacks the energy.

I have just reread the Journal which now contains (on separate sheets) both my and Charlotte's comments. I have not the strength to say much more about it, only that Charlotte and I often disagreed on many things, and one of them was Emily. Charlotte always saw her as a true heroine, even when Emily was sullen, or angry, or impossibly selfish. And since her death, she has elevated her to a pedestal worthy of a saint. I can imagine Emily looking down on her and saying 'Charlotte, you silly goose, don't you remember your lanky, naughty sister? Don't you remember how I used to tease you and lead you into bogs, and make a joke of your big head and short legs?' I loved

Emily as much as anyone could, but I also saw her faults which were legion. I miss her now more than I can say, but it is a disservice to her memory to forget that she was only human, after all.

If only spring would come, and I could get on with my work.

A. Brontë

---

23 March 1849

Today I had a kind and compassionate note from dear Ellen Nussey. She has invited me to spend several weeks with her at Brookroyd in the hopes that this will aid in my recovery. Alas, I fear it is now too late to hope for such an optimistic outcome, but I was deeply moved by her generous offer. And it has made me think of other possibilities. There is one place in all the world which I would love to see again before I die — Scarborough and the sea. Some of the happiest days of my life were spent there, in spite of the Robinsons, and I would very much like to see it again, and perhaps recover a memory of the joy of those times. I shall ask Charlotte to write to Ellen and suggest that the two of them accompany me.

AB

---

5 April 1849

I am very cross with Charlotte. She is, I find, much more selfish than I had ever realized. Of course I always knew that she loved Emily better than she loved me, but that she would deny me one last pleasure in life simply to avoid offending Ellen Nussey — well, I am very disappointed, to say the least. And I find it very hard to sympathize with her melodramatic grief over Emily's loss. For a time the bereavement brought us together, but now it divides us.

I have written to Dr. Teale in Leeds for his opinion on the advisability of my spending several weeks at the seaside; surely Charlotte will not go against his advice.

AB

---

15 April 1849

I am delighted to report that Dr. Teale has seconded my plea for an extended visit to Scarborough, and he suggests that six or eight weeks might be long enough to secure a substantial extension to my life. I fear he is being too hopeful, but I know it will do me good. And Charlotte has finally agreed to accompany me, though rather grudgingly, thanks to Papa's insistence that he is quite well enough to be left alone for a few months, with only Martha and Tabby to look after him at home, and Mr. Nicholls to aid him in his clerical duties. She has promised to write to Ellen and suggest that we all three travel to Scarborough at the earliest opportunity.

AB

---

1 May 1849

Charlotte continues to drag her heels in arranging the trip to Scarborough! My health continues very poor, and I grow thinner every day. Can she not see that every delay decreases what possible benefits this sojourn might bring? Now it is put off until late May. I fear it may be too late.

AB

---

22 May 1849

At last! We leave for Scarborough tomorrow, all being well. Ellen will meet us at Leeds, and we continue by rail to York (the

Minster!) and then on to S. I am fair dizzy with excitement. I know I am in God's Hands and am confident that He will allow me this one last great pleasure before I take my leave of this world.

Anne Brontë

Anne died on the 28th of May, peacefully and in the certain hope of the life to come. I remained with Ellen in Scarbro' for a week, in order to deal with all the practical and tiresome matters connected with the funeral and the burial. Anne had requested that she be buried there, in the churchyard of St Mary's, and now at last I understand why she had desired this and was so very insistent on visiting this town — she wanted to die there. It is an inspiringly beautiful place and I think it is far better that she rest in a peaceful and serene churchyard near the sea than to be buried under the gloomy pavement of Haworth Church.

Ellen and I spent a quiet time in Filey, recovering from the stresses and strains of the last weeks, and now I am at home again.

I have read over this Journal for the last time; now I must bow to Emily's and Anne's wishes, and destroy it. I own that the temptation to keep it is very enticing, but I will be strong. It would be unthinkable for it to fall into the wrong hands after my death.

So, farewell, Emily my love. Farewell, Anne. Perhaps 'we three shall meet again' in a better place. We were always the three weird sisters, and bonds stronger than blood held us even when we went our separate ways. Now Currer, Acton, and Ellis must stand in our places and let the Bells toll on after we are no more.

C. Brontë

The Brontë Parsonage
(Author's photograph)

Built in 1778 and occupied by the perpetual curates of Haworth: John Richardson (1763 – 91), James Charnock (1791 – 1819), and Patrick Brontë (1820 – 61).

The Brontë Parsonage
(Author's photograph)

Springhead from the front
(Author's photograph)

The home of the family of Joseph Greenwood, Esq., J.P., from the time of his marriage to Grace Cockcroft (c1810) to his bankruptcy in 1853. All his five children were born there: William Cockcroft (1811), James (1813), Sarah (1816), Martha (1818), and Anne (1820).

Springhead from the side
(Author's photograph)

B r i d g e h o u s e
(Author's photograph)

The ancestral home of the Greenwoods of Haworth, probably
built in the 17th century and renovated extensively in the 1740s.

Woodlands
(Author's photograph)

Built in about 1832 by John and James Greenwood, the brothers of Joseph of Springhead. After John's death in 1833, the house became the family home of James, his wife and two children. Located well away from the main street and also from the family's mills, the front entrance is accessible only by a long drive. Like Bridgehouse and Springhead, it is a gentleman's residence located in a valley; thus all three Greenwood houses have features in common with Thrushcross Grange in *Wuthering Heights.*

Woodlands, rear access
(Author's photograph)

This almost concealed opening in Stubbings Lane (now Sun Street) permits access to the stable yard of Woodlands, and indirectly to the rear of the house. (Author's photograph)

Ponden Hall

Ancestral home of the Heaton family
Early photograph
(Courtesy of the Brontë Society)

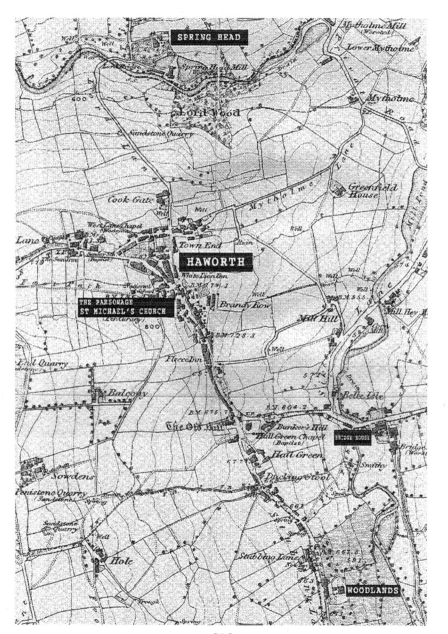

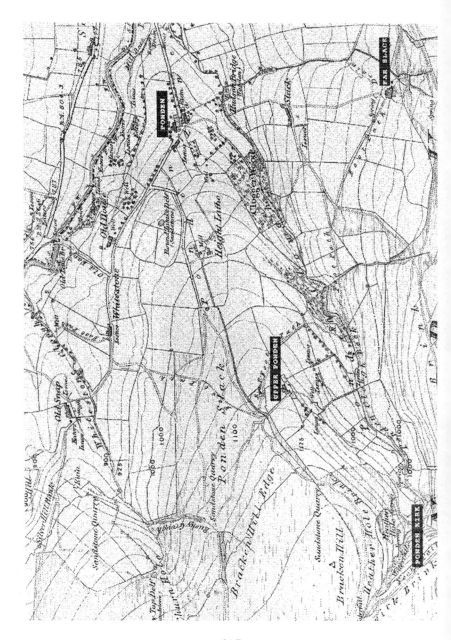

217

Grasper – from life by Emily Brontë

January 1834. Pencil on paper
(Courtesy of the Brontë Society)

Keeper – from life by Emily Brontë

24 April 1838. Watercolour on paper.
(Courtesy of the Brontë Society)

Flossy by Emily Brontë

c. 1843. Watercolour on paper.
(Courtesy of the Brontë Society)

**Keeper, Flossy and Tiger
by Emily Brontë**

1843. Watercolour.
(Courtesy of the Brontë Society)

Afterword

The theory that Emily Brontë loved and lost a young man of working class origins while in her teens was developed from several strands of fact and circumstantial evidence which appear to complement each other, and to suggest the plausibility of the conclusion. The basic elements of the theory were constructed from the following pieces of evidence:

1) The letter of July, 1835, from Patrick Brontë to Mrs. James Franks expressing anxiety over his daughters' moral character as they are about to depart for Roe Head School.

2) The striking change of tone in Emily's poetry between 1836 and 1837 from dreamy speculation on the future ('Will the day be bright or cloudy?' July 12, 1836) and a joyous evocation of nature ('High waving heather...' December 13, 1836) to an outpouring of poetry concerned with grief and death beginning in early 1837. Also striking are the many references in Emily's poetry to an early tragedy which changed and aged her.

3) The apparent change in Emily's character between her school year at Cowan Bridge ('the pet nursling of the school', 'reads very prettily'), and her later reputation as cold and reserved.

4) Various aspects of Emily's one novel, *Wuthering Heights*, which seem to be based indirectly on personal experience.

5) The discovery that:
   a) a young man, Robert Clayton (1818 – 36), the son of a weaver, lived and died at a time and place consonant with the theory,

b) his initials are found next to one of Emily's poems, and

c) the deaths of Robert and his brother John appear to be reflected in at least two of Emily's poems.

Most of the material relating to the Greenwood families of Springhead, Bridgehouse, and Woodlands is based on documentary evidence, although the extension of this to support a theoretical relationship between Emily Brontë and James Greenwood is entirely hypothetical. However, it is plausible in the context of what is known about the connections between the Brontë family and the various Greenwood families (see below).

The incidents described in the Journal or in the Annotations which are almost entirely fabricated or based on hearsay (in addition to the scenes directly connected with the basic theory) are:

1) The death of Grasper.
2) The introduction of Keeper to the family.
3) The details of Emily's first menstrual period.
4) The psychic communication between Emily and Anne in 1837.
5) Mellaney Hayne's communication with the Brontës after they left Cowan Bridge in 1825.
6) Models for Heathcliff: Dr. William Scoresby and Frederick Douglass.
7) The consultation with Mr. Butterfield in early 1848, and Emily's decision not to write another novel.
8) The meeting with Mr. Thos Newby in London (July, 1848).
9) Charlotte's footnote concerning black slaves in Yorkshire and Westmorland.

The first and second of these incidents must have occurred, however, simply because we know that Grasper seems to have disappeared some time between 1834, when Emily painted his likeness from life, and 1838 when she did a similar likeness of Keeper. It is fairly safe to assume that there was not a long period of time between the loss of Grasper and the advent of Keeper.

223

The third occurrence, the onset of Emily's menstrual periods, has been included mainly because it inevitably must have happened, and it is something that any teenage girl would have remarked on in her diary or journal. The supposition that this may have contributed to Emily's famous antipathy to doctors seemed particularly plausible, but of course there is no documentary evidence of this. Certainly there could have been many possible reasons for it, and it could be related to the time her arm was cut in 1833, and even to the deaths of her sisters, Maria and Elizabeth, in 1825.

The fourth incident, the psychic communication between Anne and Emily in the late spring of 1837, was included for several reasons, but there is no evidence that such a thing ever happened. However, it is known that the two girls were extremely close, at least in the early days. It is also known that Charlotte defended the similar event in *Jane Eyre*, when Jane and Rochester both hear the other calling to them from many miles away; according to Mrs. Gaskell, Charlotte said categorically that 'it is a true thing; it really happened.' Mrs. Gaskell also comments that 'I do not know what incident was in Miss Brontë's recollection when she replied.' Although there are instances of similar mystical communications in Charlotte's juvenilia, and in various novels she may have read, the words, 'it really happened' (if reported accurately) suggest that it either happened to herself, or to people very close to her, and was not something she merely made up or read about.

The fifth item on the list concerns Mellaney Hayne, the Brontë girls' close school-friend at Cowan Bridge. A considerable amount of circumstantial evidence points to the likelihood that correspondence between Charlotte and Mellaney did continue after the Brontë girls left the Clergy Daughters' School at Cowan Bridge in 1825. In the 1840s Mellaney's sister Augusta married a clergyman from Jamaica whose first wife had been a Creole, the daughter of a successful plantation owner on the island. The similarity to Rochester's first wife, Bertha Mason, seems too close to be a coincidence. And Mellaney had other connections which seem to point to her later influence on the Brontës; her sister-in-law really was a cousin of Byron and Augusta Leigh. This lady, Emma Eardley Wilmot, was also related by marriage to Captain William Edward Parry, one of the heroes of the early Brontë juvenilia, and a particular hero of Emily. And there is also a strong possibility that Mellaney may herself have had a Byron connection; although this cannot be proved beyond doubt, she may have been governess to the daughters of the Countess of Gosford, a Patroness of the Clergy Daughters' School, and a close lifelong friend of Annabella Milbanke, Lady Byron.

Regarding the possibility that Emily may have been interested in Dr. Scoresby (number 6), there is certainly no documentary evidence for this. However there is evidence to suggest that Dr. Scoresby was surprisingly friendly with the Brontë family. Not only did he request, in a letter to Mr. Grant of 1846, that both Charlotte and Mr. Brontë be included in the Grammar School Trustees' dinner with the Cranmers and himself, he also spoke later to at least two people about Haworth and the Brontës: to Mr. John Abbott in 1851, and to Mrs. Gaskell in 1855. One might also logically assume that the fact that he was a famous Arctic explorer and scientist must have interested Emily, given her early fascination with Captain Wm Edward Parry. But the idea that Dr. Scoresby may have influenced Emily's conception of Heathcliff comes from a description of Scoresby in *Barrow's Boys* by Fergus Fleming (1998): 'Physically, he [Scoresby] was striking, even sinister-looking. Although slight, he was enormously strong, and possessed of a stamina that seems unimaginable nowadays... His face was that of a gypsy, high cheekbones, dark skin, pointed nose and chin, thin lips, black curly hair. His eyes held a force that even he did not understand. Once, as an experiment, he decided to outstare a ship's dog. The beast, reckoned to be the most savage of its kind, ran back and forth snarling in panic as Scoresby approached, before finally jumping overboard and drowning.' Dr. Scoresby was in fact extremely adept as an amateur hypnotist. This was at a time when there was quite a craze for this phenomenon, as Charlotte was well aware. Whether he ever practised his hypnotic talents on any of the Brontës is not known, but there is no denying that he was very attractive to the opposite sex, and his natural 'animal magnetism' undoubtedly played its part.

225

That Emily was influenced in her creation of Heathcliff by the famous mullato Abolitionist, Frederick Douglass, is, of course, entirely hypothetical. It is possible, however, as he was in the British Isles from late summer, 1845, to the spring of 1847, and spoke at several venues in Yorkshire in the summer of 1846. And anyone gazing on the photograph of the young Mr. Douglass at the age of 17, may experience a sudden frisson of recognition — this is what Heathcliff must have looked like!

The seventh point concerns Emily's supposed visit to Mr. Francis Butterfield in Wilsden. This is based on an anecdote in Harry Speight's *History of Bingley* (1898). Mr. Butterfield himself recounted the incident to Mr. Speight in a version differing from that which appears in Emily's Journal entry, but there are several reasons to believe the Journal entry more likely to be accurate. Mr. Butterfield says that it was Charlotte who made the long trek to Wilsden from Haworth, accompanied by 'her dog, "Floss", to 'consult [him] with respect to a proposed story on the Chartist Agitation'. This strikes me as highly unlikely. Charlotte was known not to be a particularly strong walker, and the distance from Haworth across the moors to Wilsden is at least six miles. Emily, on the other hand, was a good walker, and enjoyed walking out with the dogs. Furthermore, Mr. Butterfield's claim, according to Mr. Speight, that he and Charlotte discussed her next novel would have been impossible as at that time (1848), no one yet knew that Charlotte Brontë was the novelist, Currer Bell, or that she had ever written anything for publication. My suggestion that it was Emily who went to see Mr. Butterfield, pretending to be acting on behalf of Branwell (who was well-known in the area as a published poet), makes more sense. I suspect that Mr. Butterfield reinterpreted what had happened *after* the publication of *Shirley*, when it became known that Currer Bell was Charlotte Brontë, and he then assumed that the Miss Brontë he had met that day was Charlotte. According to Speight, Butterfield told 'Miss Brontë' that such a work would only fan the 'still smouldering embers of discontent', and when they parted he claims 'she said, "I shall act upon your advice".' If it is true that the Miss Brontë who visited Mr. Butterfield was actually Emily, and not Charlotte, this remark could be the proof needed to settle the vexed question of whether Emily wrote a second novel.

Regarding the trip to London by Charlotte and Anne to clarify their identities to their publishers in July, 1848, this is largely documented in a letter Charlotte wrote to Mary Taylor in New Zealand (4 September 1848). Although this letter gives an excellent picture of the meeting with Mr. Smith and Mr. Williams of the firm Smith, Elder, it does not relate what happened when the two girls went on to visit Thomas Cautley Newby. Charlotte's letter ends with the words, 'We saw Newby — but of him more another time. Good by — God bless you — write CB'. As the meeting with Newby was of critical importance to Emily, it was absolutely necessary that some account of it be included in the Journal annotations. The idea that there had been a previous agreement between the girls to maintain the fiction that Ellis Bell was a man, brother of Currer and Acton, seems wholly logical under the circumstances.

Lastly, Charlotte's account of rumours relating to the slaves of Dent Dale and Storrs Hall refer to rumours about which I have read, or heard by word of mouth. I have not invented them, but I cannot vouch for their truth. But the Brontë girls may very well have heard the same rumours as I.

A Few Words Regarding the Background of Several Entries

The Dog Bite Incident

The entry in which Emily describes her and Robert's adventure at Woodlands, where they are pursued by the dogs (and Emily is bitten, thus becoming infected with erysipelas), is based on a remarkable conjunction of fact and plausible speculation: it is a documented fact that Emily contracted erysipelas in the late summer of 1833 (letter from Charlotte Brontë to Ellen Nussey, 11 September 1833). The probability that this was caused by a dog bite is highly likely. It is also a documented fact that Emily was bitten by a dog at some time and cauterized the wound herself (Charlotte to Mrs. Gaskell) and this event was used by Charlotte in *Shirley*, a novel whose title character is known to be

227

based on Emily. Furthermore, it is a fact that the elegant new house, Woodlands, was finished in about 1832, and really was the home of James and Hannah Greenwood and their two young sons. And it is also a fact that there was enmity between James Greenwood and Patrick Brontë; besides religious and political differences, James Greenwood opposed the appointment of his brother, Joseph, as magistrate in the mid-1830s, while Patrick Brontë championed Joseph's cause (see Barker, J., *The Brontës*). This would explain why Emily had not previously seen the house (had Mr. Brontë and Mr. Greenwood been friendly, the two families would have been on visiting terms) and why she and Robert were so afraid of being discovered. Lastly, the parallel scene in *Wuthering Heights,* in which Cathy and Heathcliff spy on the Lintons at Thrushcross Grange and Cathy is bitten by the dog Skulker, allows a direct connection to be made between the theory, the known facts, and the novel itself. In other words, though we have no proof that such an incident took place, it is highly plausible from many points of view.

The Party at Springhead, Spring, 1836

The credibility of this scene is based on the relationship between Joseph Greenwood, his family, and the Brontës; the nature of Haworth society; and the timing of the event.

I cannot emphasize strongly enough the importance of the related Greenwood families of Bridgehouse, Woodlands, and Springhead in the social hierarchy of Haworth. Descended from a long line of entrepreneurs in the area, by the early 19th century this family was the wealthiest in the neighbourhood, and socially the best connected. There were also thriving branches of the family in Oxenhope and East Morton, but the Haworth branch, the senior line, owned and operated the largest spinning mill in the town (Bridgehouse Mills); they were also the largest landowners. When old James Greenwood of Bridgehouse died in 1824, he left a large estate and settled £4,000 (or the equivalent in real estate) on each of his four daughters, while the sons, John, James, and Joseph, inherited the business and/or the real estate. (It was actually a lot more complicated than this, but not worth describing in detail.) They were also related to, and very friendly with, the Greenwoods of Keighley who were at that time the wealthiest family in the entire larger area.

Martha Clapham Greenwood (1766 – 1831), the wife of the above James Greenwood (1763 – 1824), was Haworth's leading society matron in her time, and is known to have been friendly with the Brontë family when they first came to Haworth, according to Mrs. Gaskell. The incident described in the Journal in which Mrs. Greenwood upbraids Charlotte for rudeness to her Aunt derives from a true story passed down in the Greenwood family. When Mrs. Greenwood died, she was buried beside her husband; their tomb is probably the largest monument in the Haworth graveyard. The inscription reads:

'Sacred to the Memory of ... Martha Greenwood... who departed this life Nov. 23rd 1831, in the 66th year of her AGE, having fulfilled all the duties of the domestic Life with assiduity and uprightness — those of the social state in the spirit of pure philanthropy and the sacred duties of Religion, with unfeigned humility and unwavering perseverance. In her the cause of God had a munificent and constant supporter, The poor and distressed a patron and benefactor, the young a wise counsellor, and all a sincere friend. She lived universally respected, and died deeply lamented — peacefully committing her Soul into the hand of her much loved Lord, and unchangeable Saviour.'

It is interesting to note that this monumental inscription is on the tombstone and not on a plaque inside the Church. This is undoubtedly because the Greenwoods were Strict Baptists, not Church of England. The only one of James and Martha Greenwood's sons who was an Anglican was Joseph Greenwood; and he and his entire family are all buried under the floor of the Church. Their marble memorial plaque is now located in the wall at the rear of the new Church, but before the old Church was rebuilt in 1881, the plaque was located inside the Communion Rail, a position of highest honour.

It is evident that this family was socially highly placed; in 1833 Joseph Greenwood became the Lord of the Manor of

Oxenhope, a title purchased from Thomas Egerton, the Earl of Wilton (and younger brother of the Marquess of Westminster, Richard Grosvenor). From 1834 Joseph was Chairman of the Church Land Trustees, and required to be present at every vestry meeting. In 1836 he was appointed by the Lord Lieutenant of Yorkshire, Lord Harewood, as Haworth's first local magistrate. This was achieved in large part by the efforts of Mr. Brontë, who wished to ensure that a Tory and Churchman gained the post, and not a Whig or Dissenter (see Barker, *The Brontës*, Chapters 8 and 9). But Joseph Greenwood and Patrick Brontë had a great deal more in common than religion and politics; both men had lost their wives within a year of each other, neither ever remarried, and their daughters were exactly the same ages. Joseph also had two sons — William Cockcroft (1811 – 56) and James (1813 – 89). Sadly, Joseph's middle daughter, Martha (1818 – 76), was probably mentally unstable, but there is documentary evidence that the youngest daughter, Ann (1820 – 38), was friendly with the Brontë sisters; a letter of 22 July, 1836 reads as follows:

To Miss A Greenwood Spring Head

My dear Anne

Should the weather prove favourable we shall be very happy to wait upon yourself and Sister at the time mentioned in your note — which I presume from the date is this afternoon.

I am affectionately Your
C Brontë

Only one of Anne's sisters is mentioned as the eldest sister, Sarah (b. 1816) had died in May, 1833. There is a small water colour in the Brontë Parsonage of Sarah ('Miss Greenwood') thought to be by either Charlotte or Emily Brontë. The provenance is fairly good, as the picture almost certainly came originally from Sarah's brother James (Emily Brontë's hypothetical suitor) by a short chain of owners, no more than four, by gift or inheritance, not purchase.

As to whether there actually was a party at Springhead in the spring of 1836, I have no evidence, no more can I prove that young James Greenwood ever courted Emily Brontë. But the shadow of such a figure may possibly be seen dimly in Charlotte's introduction to the 1850 edition of *Wuthering Heights*: '...for an example of constancy and tenderness, remark that of Edgar Linton. (Some people will think these qualities do not shine so well incarnate in a man as they would do in a woman, but Ellis Bell [Emily] could never be brought to comprehend this notion: nothing moved her more than any insinuation that the faithfulness and clemency, the long-suffering and loving-kindness which are esteemed virtues in the daughters of Eve, become foibles in the sons of Adam. She held that mercy and forgiveness are the divinest attributes of the Great Being who made both man and woman, and that which clothes the Godhead in glory, can disgrace no form of feeble humanity.)'

This comment strongly suggests that Emily's opinion was more than hypothetical, and that she knew a young man of this description. Whether or not this person was young James Greenwood is impossible to say for certain. But, given the strong resemblance between the Linton family and the family of Joseph Greenwood, and the close relations between this family and the Brontës, I think the identification of James Greenwood with Edgar Linton is not too far-fetched.

It might be objected that James's brother William would have been an equally good choice, but there is enough known about William to reject him: he reverted to the Baptist faith and was a good friend of Mr. Brontë's opponent, William Winterbotham, the Baptist minister; and he was known to be fat; both of these facts are recorded by Branwell Brontë in a letter to the sexton, John Brown. In addition, to judge from several letters of his to his lawyer and to his father (in the Calderdale Archives), he was self-pitying, greedy, and generally unpleasant. Sadly, all I could find out about James Greenwood was that he looked after his lunatic sister Martha until her death in 1876, he never married, and he left most of his money to charity.

One more point of resemblance between the Lintons and the various Greenwoods, besides their wealth and social standing, is the location of their homes: Bridgehouse,

Woodlands, and Spring Head, like Thrushcross Grange, are all large, elegant houses of relatively recent date (18th or early 19th century) located in valleys. This is in contrast to the elevated situation of, for example, the two old houses at Ponden, Far Slack, the three Withins, and Upper Ponden, all of which have locations more similar to that of Wuthering Heights. It is possible that the great importance Emily Brontë attached to the locations of the residences of the Earnshaws and the Lintons may reflect more than just a literary device.

Tabitha Ackroyd's Accident

In constructing the theoretical sequence of events for those climactic days of the 12th to the 17th of December, 1836, I have used Emily's amazing poem of the 13th ('High waving heather...'), the funeral of Robert Clayton on the 14th of December (recorded in the Haworth Parish Records), and Charlotte Brontë's letters to Ellen Nussey of the 14th and 29th of December.

There is only one contemporary source for Tabby's accident, but it is completely authentic. This is Charlotte's letter to Ellen Nussey of the 29th of December, 1836. '...I have a sufficient and very melancholy excuse [for not writing sooner] in an accident that befell our old faithful Tabby a few days after my return home...' Charlotte and Anne returned home from Roe Head on the 14th of December (letter from Charlotte to Ellen Nussey, 14 Dec. 1836, '...on this day we all go HOME.'). But the letter of the 29th presents several difficulties, which, I suggest, support the theory that there was another problem at home, other than Tabby's accident, which prevented Charlotte from writing to Ellen for such a long time (two weeks), and that this problem may have been Emily's traumatized state. It is clear from Charlotte's letter of the 14th that she intends to write to Ellen as soon as she gets home as she is hoping Ellen will come to Haworth, presumably before Christmas. That this letter was never written suggests that Charlotte was confronted with another crisis immediately on her return, *before* Tabby's

232

accident which happened 'a few days after' her return. Turning to the actual text of the letter of the 29th, Charlotte's tone is strangely illogical; it is almost hysterical. This could be explained simply by her disappointment in not seeing Ellen and by worry about Tabby, but one sentence at least suggests a deeper disturbance: 'After this disappointment I never dare reckon with certainty of the enjoyment of a pleasure again... it seems as if some fatality stood between you and me, I am not good enough for you, and you must be kept from contamination of too intimate society.' Charlotte then goes on to give another reason why Ellen must not come ('Should Tabby die while you are in the house... I should never forgive myself...'), although she has already given several perfectly adequate reasons in the previous paragraphs (lack of household help and the icy weather). This overkill of excuses suggests that in fact the real reason that Ellen must not come cannot be named, and it might well be the disturbing condition of Charlotte's sister Emily.

The entry in the Journal recounting the conversation between Tabby and Emily in the kitchen on the evening of the 12th, however, is entirely hypothetical, and was needed in order to provide Emily with a state of mind conducive to the writing of 'High waving heather...' her poem of the 13th of December. It was only after I had written this that I realized it was very similar to the exchange between Catherine Earnshaw and Nellie Dean the night Heathcliff overhears Catherine say she could never marry him as they would be poor (Chap. 9). Either I was subconsciously using that passage to underpin the theory, or the theory is true and actually explains why Emily wrote that scene in *Wuthering Heights*. The truth in this case is certainly a mystery to me.

What Happened at Law Hill?

Emily's position as a teacher at Law Hill School, 1838 – 39, is a matter of record. However, the details of how she obtained the post and what happened during her short period of employment there are unknown. Until recently even the date and duration of her posting were a subject of controversy. That it definitely was 1838 – 39 is now a well-established fact (Chitham, *A Life of Emily Brontë*, 1987, and Cox, *Brontë Society Transactions*, 1984), but the reason for her departure remains vague. Mrs. Gaskell says it may have been for reasons of health, and Mrs. Chadwick (*In the Footsteps of the Brontës*, 1914) simply says that the family decided she should be at home. My 'invention', that she was dismissed for insubordination, seems to me as likely a reason as any, and more likely than most; she was known to have a warm temper, and not to suffer fools. However it is just possible that she was summoned home that spring as both her sisters found employment. On the other hand, the reverse may be true — that only after Emily came home, for whatever reason, did Charlotte apparently feel pressured to accept the temporary post of governess to the Sidgwicks of Stonegappe. Emily was at home at least by April, 1839, and probably as early as March, when she writes her first poem since the Christmas holidays. Charlotte certainly found her post *after* April, 1839, to judge by her letter of the 15th of April to Ellen Nussey which simply says 'I am as yet "wanting a situation...".' Her first letter to Emily from Stonegappe is dated the 8th of June.

As to how Emily obtained the post, whether she was asked to teach piano, and whether she was required to read to the young boarders, all the answers to these questions are hypothetical. However, it is known that she considered herself very overworked (Charlotte's letter to Ellen of the 2nd of October, 1838: 'I have had one letter from [Emily] since her departure...it gives an appalling account of her duties...') and Mrs. Watkinson, a former pupil of Emily's at Law Hill, told Mrs. Chadwick that 'her [Emily's] work was hard as she had not the faculty of doing it quickly'. Furthermore, Emily produced no poetry in early 1839, whereas there are a large number of poems written in the autumn and early winter of 1838. This suggests that her limited free time became even more limited on her return to Law Hill in January, and this supports the assumption that Emily was given more duties of some sort at that time.

Emily's Confrontation with the Beggars, March, 1843

This episode is drawn from a variety of sources, including my own research. Although there is no evidence that Emily actually confronted a rebellious or hostile crowd, there is plenty of evidence that this situation could have arisen. 1842 had been a year of riot and rebellion in the manufacturing districts of Great Britain, and Charlotte's footnote referring to the Plug Riots is accurate. It is also a fact that Patrick Brontë was in York for the Assizes in March, 1843; the crime described in the Journal was a real one, and on the reverse of the giant sheet recording the case in the Public Record Office are the names of the sworn witnesses, one of whom, along with Joseph Greenwood and William Thomas, is Patrick Brontë. We also know that at this time Mr. Brontë visited his son and daughter at Thorp Green, home of the Robinsons, which is not far from York. Local Leeds papers reveal that 50 special constables were appointed in Haworth just before the time Patrick Brontë, Joseph Greenwood, and William Thomas were to be away from Haworth for the York Assizes. And we know from the diary note of John Greenwood, the Haworth stationer (no relation to the Greenwoods described above), that Emily was taught by her father to shoot a pistol. The reason I have elaborated this story to include a confrontation between Emily and a group of beggars while she was in charge at the Parsonage is that I feel there must have been some real reason why Emily was described by her father as 'a brave and noble girl' and by her sister as a heroine. Charlotte Brontë's characterization of her eponymous heroine, Shirley, known to be a portrait of Emily ('had she been placed in health and prosperity'), reflects a sensible, strong-minded young woman, deeply concerned with the welfare of the poor. In Chapter 14 Shirley says: 'I cannot forget, either day or night, that these embittered feelings of the poor against the rich have been generated in suffering: they would neither hate nor envy us if they did not deem us so much happier than themselves.' Surely Emily herself, at some time, must have addressed the question of rich and poor, mill owners and operatives, and it seems to me highly plausible that she experienced at first hand the antagonism of the poor.

I could go on justifying my imaginative reconstruction of events as described in the Journal and the hypothetical opinions and attitudes of the three Brontë sisters, but this would descend into the special pleading I wished to avoid. However, I strongly recommend to the interested reader, if he wishes to judge for himself the plausibility of what is contained in this book, that he consult the basic texts on which it is based: first and foremost are the *Poems of Emily Brontë* (Derek Roper, Clarendon Press, 1994), and *Wuthering Heights*, of course. There are dozens of editions of the novel now available, both in paper and hardback. The other important resources are: *The Life of Charlotte Brontë* (Elizabeth Gaskell, 1857, available in the well-footnoted Oxford Univ. Press World Classics Edition,1996), *The Brontës* (Juliet Barker, Weidenfeld, 1994), *The Letters of Charlotte Brontë* (ed. Margaret Smith, Clarendon Press, vol I,, 1995, and vol II, 2000), *A Life of Emily Brontë* (Edward Chitham, Basil Blackwell, 1987), and, to a lesser extent, *In the Footsteps of the Brontës* (Mrs. Ellis Chadwick, Pitman, 1914). Many other books were consulted but these are by far the most important. In addition, my own original research articles are to be found in the *Brontë Society Transactions* (now called *Brontë Studies*). The major piece of actual evidence, however, is not to be found in any publication until now: the births and deaths of John and Robert Clayton are recorded in the Haworth Parish Registers. Additional information on the Clayton family came from census records, land tax records, deed registrations, etc., and the family's early Quaker background is described in *The History of Stanbury*, by Joseph Craven (The Rydal Press, Keighley, 1907).